The Miami Disclosure

by

Anne Downie

First published in Great Britain in 2021
by SNB Publishing Limited. 57, Orrell Lane,
Liverpool L9 8BX

Copyright 2021 Anne Downie

This is a work of fiction. Names, characters, businesses, places, events, locales, and incidents are either the products of the author's imagination or used in a fictitious manner. Any resemblance to actual persons, living or dead, or actual events is purely coincidental.

The right of Anne Downie to be identified as the author of this book has been asserted by him in accordance with the Copyright, Design and Patent Act 1988.

All rights reserved. No part of this publication may be reproduced or distributed in any form or by any means, or stored in a database or retrieval system without the prior, written permission of SNB Publishing Limited.

Other titles by the same author

Novel
The Witches of Pollok — Capercaillie Books

Plays
Waiting on One — FairPlay Press
Parking Lot In Pittsburgh — FairPlay Press
The White Bird Passes — FairPlay Press
The Yellow on the Broom — FairPlay Press
The Witches of Pollok — FairPlay Press
The Female of the Species — FairPlay Press
Cracked — S.H.E.G. Publications
Ashes to Ashes — S.H.E.G. Publications

Numerous short stories published by Polygon, The Herald and Argyle publications.

Dedication

*To my wonderful children Mark and Susan,
and in loving memory of my late husband John Downie.*

Chapter one

His foot had gone to sleep. The struggle to keep his eyes open had, somehow, transferred itself to his size twelves. Don gently tapped his foot on the floor and shook his leg, causing the woman in the next seat to give him a wary look. Unfortunately, it was the leg closest to her thigh. Broadway theatre seats were a little on the cosy side. She looked suspiciously at the jacket covering his lap. He hastily moved the offending leg away from her, as far as the cramped space would allow. At least he hadn't fallen asleep. As an Arts Correspondent, you were a marked man; nodding off at a production of *The Seagull* was even more ignominious than being thought a pervert.

He thought it the worst production he'd ever seen. He'd been sneaking surreptitious glances at his watch throughout, cursing its lack of an illuminated dial. To be fair, he had never been a great fan of Chekhov's writing. He felt the Russian was a pill you had to swallow to be thought cultured. Medication that didn't taste too great, but, judging from the hushed tones and reverence emanating from the literati, considered good for you. When he'd said this in a tutorial to Professor Greenbaum, during his student days at Yale, Don thought the great man had suffered a stroke. The old academic was so incensed; temporarily robbed of the power of speech. Don had a vague, half-formulated idea for a book, *Contemporary Criticism: The Classics*. After all, modern playwrights were often subjected to a savaging. Why should the so called 'classics' be above reproach? The plots were often ludicrous, the dialogue leaden, but because the plays had endured, they were given special exemption. Maybe it was easier to have a play produced then? There were certainly fewer playwrights about. Don wanted to even the playing field. Why should criticism of them be confined to the nature of the production and the ability, or not, of the actors?

Don was thinking again of his book idea when the applause

broke out. The rows in front of him were clapping with great enthusiasm. The large, burly couple on his other side, who noisily ate candies throughout, were on their feet, the man whooping. What was that about? He'd paid $120 each for a matinée seat, so it must be good? Don rose abruptly. He'd better watch. At twenty seven years of age, he was turning into an old cynic. He, apologetically, made his way along the row, before the actors could come back on again for a second bow. The play had lasted almost three hours, full of endless floor washing and other tedious bits of theatrical business that seemed utterly pointless. The Director had been brought over, at great expense, from Eastern Europe. Don had been told, off the record, by the Stage Manager, an old friend, that, on the first day of rehearsals, Mr Bukovski had sent the cast out to find mushrooms growing in a wood. When asked why, he had said cryptically, 'Is important you smell the mushrooms.'

Don should have guessed the production would reflect that kind of pretension.

He pushed through the exit door, his appearance surprising the young theatre attendants whose hands were still grasping the handles, expecting the audience to be in their seats. The tuxedoed House Manager smiled, with a hint of anxiety.

'Don, when will your review…?'

'Thursday,' said Don, not breaking his step. He was already running late He didn't want to become involved in a conversation. His review would say it all.

He exited into a thronged Times Square and checked his cell phone. A text from Kay flashed up. Her flight was on time. He rang his mother's mobile. It rang out. He smiled, ruefully; it was their Christmas present to her. Don't know why they'd bothered. In the six months since then, she'd never answered it. It was either 'Oh, I didn't have it out with me' or 'by the time I found it in my bag, it had stopped.'

Myra had never really embraced technology. Joe, his father, had a laptop, but his mother refused to touch it. Even her friend, Ella, couldn't persuade her to join the Silver Surfers. Ella was now happily emailing her son in Australia, exchanging photographs. Myra, though admiring of her friend's skill, was not tempted. She'd managed for sixty-eight years without it. Don left a message asking, apologetically, if they could take a cab to the restaurant, explaining he was behind schedule. He headed for his hire car, cursing the fact that he was going to hit the home-going traffic, thanks to Bukovski's self-indulgence.

Chapter two

Kay was feeling hot, sticky and unclean. The latter wasn't due, entirely, to the unseasonably warm weather, but the presence of Senator Wesley, whose considerable girth had blocked her way in the aisle of the plane.

'Well, well, Miss Prentice. We must stop meeting like this.'

He did not even make the effort to be original. She gritted her teeth and tried to be pleasant. When she'd tried to interview Wesley at the Washington Conference, the Senator had been so obnoxious, taking every innocent remark as a double entendre, that she'd walked away. Someone must tell these guys that power is a turn on, she reckoned. Even if you're repulsive, you can score! Wesley wasn't the brightest - perhaps he thought 'Me Too' was an invitation! She'd seen him in the Washington terminal, but had avoided him. Now there was no escaping. His corpulent, sweaty body was hurrying along beside her down the Arrivals corridor. Copious amounts of his pungent aftershave were not entirely successful in masking his body odour.

'I feel you've been avoiding me.'

'Really Senator?' she lied. 'I don't know what makes you think that.'

'Don't deny it. You've been giving me the brush off all week.' He smiled an oily smile. 'You want an in-depth interview, Miss Prentice, you're going to have to make amends.'

'How do I do that?'

He put a restraining hand on her arm and bent down. His mouth almost at her ear, he whispered.

'I have a house in the Hamptons. Join me this weekend.'

'Good. I look forward to meeting your wife. I take it Mrs Wesley would be joining us?' she asked with mock innocence.

'And spoil our fun?' he said suggestively.

Kay felt her gorge and anger rise at the same time. She drew herself up, looked witheringly at his corpulent body.

'Sorry Senator, I save whales. I don't screw 'em.'

She walked away, leaving Wesley open-mouthed, his expression quickly changing as he became aware of cameramen and reporters at the barrier.

....

Don talked into a small recorder as he walked from the car-park. The review had crystallised in his mind on the journey to LaGuardia.

'Chekhov claimed the play was a comedy. Unfortunately, this production is more Greek tragedy with samovars. One to be avoided.'

He slipped the recorder into his pocket and hurried through the airport doors, looked around, checked the board. The flight had landed fifteen minutes earlier. She wouldn't have left the building? Just then he saw her tall, elegant figure emerge from the washroom. She moved with such an easy feline grace that she could have been mistaken for a dancer. She might have been, too, if an accident, while on a junior school skiing trip, hadn't broken her leg so severely that it had put paid to any dreams of pursuing the ballet career she had nurtured from the age of five. Not that she regretted it. Kay dealt with circumstances as they were, not as they might have been. It was one of the traits he loved about her, a strong positive attitude. Kay's cup was never half-full.

He hurried towards her, kissed her. 'Sorry, I'm late, sweetheart.'

'It's ok. Gave me a chance to wash Senator Wesley off me.'

'What?'

'Don't worry. Only his paw-print.'

As they hurried out of the airport, she reached into her leather holdall and produced a gold-foiled, be-ribboned package, with a little gift tag attached. Don looked at it, slightly dismayed.

'You've wrapped it?'

'Had to. Knew we'd be cutting it fine. Left the card for you to write.' She smiled. 'Just act as if you've seen it when your Dad opens it.'

. . . .

Marco's was the kind of restaurant that lifted your spirits as soon as you entered. The warmth of the welcome; genuine Italian hospitality greeted you. You were never left standing, awkwardly, trying to catch a waiter's eye before being shown to a table. Marco seemed to be everywhere. It was as if you were a valued guest in his home. Don was not too worried at being ten minutes late. He knew his parents would be well looked after. Marco ushered Don and Kay to where they were sitting munching into complimentary appetisers; zucchini and aubergine fritters in the lightest of batters, accompanied by a dish of subtly tangy sauce. Joe and Myra were looking slightly flushed. The large Southern Comforts in front of them had obviously hit the spot. Don kissed his mother.

'Sorry, we're late. Traffic was a nightmare.'

'Happy Birthday, Joe.' Kay hugged him with a genuine affection.

Don placed the birthday present in front of his Father.

'Hope you like it. It's from both of us.'

Joe removed the wrapping paper to reveal a small box which he opened carefully. Nestling in its plush, velvet interior, lay an antique watch, a gold half-hunter. He was overwhelmed. 'This is too much.'

'It's even older than you, Dad.'

Joe hugged them both. 'Thank you. Thank you both. Never expected anything like this.'

They'd thought of a birthday cake but decided against it. Joe was the kind of man who hated drawing attention to himself. A restaurant full of strangers being obliged to sing 'Happy Birthday' was his idea of hell. They'd pitched it just right. Small intimate family dinner and he was happy.

It had been a wonderful night. Joe was still raving about his veal in cream and wild mushroom sauce, as Marco helped Myra into her coat.

Don emerged into the cool night air and opened the cab door, giving Kay a final hug before she got in.

'The watch was a great suggestion. You're a genius.'

Kay smiled. 'Tell that to our editor. He'll maybe give me a raise.'

'See you tomorrow.'

Chapter three

The New York-Connecticut freeway was, thankfully, not too busy. Mind you, it was midnight. Don couldn't understand people who said they loved driving. For him, it was merely a means of getting from A to B. Like two-thirds of New Yorkers, he didn't own a car. Sitting in traffic jams, breathing other people's exhaust fumes, was anathema to him. When he first moved to New York, he'd found it an amazing city to explore on foot, every neighbourhood a different adventure. He had never really lost that sense of wonder. True, he relied more on public transport and cabs these days, but it was worth it to avoid the congestion. He hired a car only when he needed it, like now, but he didn't particularly enjoy the experience.

It started to rain, gently at first but with increasing force. He took a hand off the wheel and rubbed his eyes. Joseph looked at him, a little concerned.

'Tired, son?'

'Just a little.'

'Told you we should have stayed over, Myra.'

'And I told you, Trixie won't settle if we leave her overnight.'

'You think more of that damn dog than you think of me!'

Don smiled. It was an argument he'd heard a hundred times. He knew there was no malice in it.

'Kay is a lovely girl. When you guys setting the date?'

'Joe!' Myra admonished 'Ignore him, Don. Subtlety was never his strong point.'

But Don didn't hear their conversation in its entirety. His eyes had momentarily closed. It hazily reminded him of the time he'd had his tonsils removed, as a child and had wakened up from the anaesthetic with the sound of voices drifting in and out of his consciousness. He came to with a jolt, realising he'd hit a patch of water. The car started to aquaplane across the road.

'Don! Watch out!'

His father's frantic tone was the last thing he heard before the collision. The truck seemed to have appeared out of nowhere. He tried desperately to swerve, but it was too late. The back of his car took the impact. He heard his mother's screams as the car rolled over three times before landing upside down on the freeway. It came to rest, wheels spinning. Don sank into merciful unconsciousness.

The truck driver, shaken but unhurt, climbed out of his vehicle and approached Don's car with trepidation. He looked inside and felt physically sick. There was blood everywhere. He had worked eight years in an abattoir in Chicago. Thought he was inured to blood, but this was different. He broke the ominous silence. 'Jesus!'

It was more prayer than expletive that he uttered.

The old couple in the back seat looked pretty far gone. The young guy, slumped over the air bag stirred and moaned.

'Hey, buddy, you ok?'
He reached for his cell phone, dialled 911.

'Hang on, man. Help's on its way.'

Other vehicles were pulling up. Drivers got out and approached, morbid curiosity overcoming their fear.

'There was nothing I could do. He was across the line.'

The truck driver repeated his defence to the motorcycle cop who was first on the scene, closely followed by an ambulance.

Don came to as he was being stretchered into the ambulance. Blood was seeping from a wound on his head. He opened his eyes for a moment to see a body bag being zipped up.

His father's antique watch, its face smashed and its frame crushed, lay on the freeway. He lapsed into unconsciousness before he could witness the frantic efforts of the rescue team to free his mother.

Chapter four

The sheets felt clean and cool. It was dark outside. For a moment he thought he was in his apartment. Then he saw an unfamiliar figure coming towards him and struggled to sit up.

'Take it easy, now.' The nurse's voice was gentle, but firm.

'Mom... Dad?'

She didn't have to say anything. He knew from her face that the news wasn't good.

'Tell me!' He hardly recognised the agitated voice that came from within him.

She hesitated for a moment. 'I'll get Doctor.' She exited.

Not knowing quite why, he struggled to get out of bed. He clutched his ribs, grimacing in pain. Doctor Rodgers, a man with dark, wiry hair and a quiet authority, despite his youth, came through the door, in time to gently lead him back to bed.

'Not a good idea Mr Creighton. You've had a nasty crack on the head. And two of your ribs are fractured.'

'What about my folks?'

He could see the momentary hesitation in the Doctor's face. The man was calculating whether his patient, in his present state, could take the truth.

'Tell me... please.'

'Your father's dead, Mr Creighton.'

Don felt as if someone had reached in and stopped his heart.

'There was nothing we could do. He was dead when they pulled him from the car. Multiple injuries. Death would have been instantaneous.'

Don scarcely dared to ask, 'And Mom?'

. . . .

Kay turned over in bed. It couldn't be morning already. Then she realised it wasn't her alarm that had wakened her. She came to with a start and picked up her phone. She could hardly take in what the cop was saying, but kept her wits together long enough to write down the name and address of the hospital. 'Thank you. Thank you so much. Tell him I'm on my way.'

Even though Don was prepared for the worst, the sight that met him made him want to weep. As the orderly wheeled him through the door of the Intensive Care Unit, he barely recognised the pale, bandaged figure lying in the bed, attached to a mass of wires. She seemed so frail. Drip tubes fed into one arm. The technology she hated seemed to be the only thing keeping his mother alive. He knew her grip on life was a tenuous one. Dr Rogers seemed to feel it was a miracle she was still alive, such was the extent of her internal injuries. Don took her hand in his, fighting back his emotions. 'Mom... It's Don... I'm here...'

The Orderly tactfully withdrew.

. . . .

Kay approached the desk. The journey to the hospital had seemed unreal, the miles barely registering. The desk clerk looked up, taking in the tall, striking looking girl, with the worried expression.

'I'm looking for a patient, Mr Creighton, Don Creighton.'

'Are you family?'

'I'm his fiancée.'

The nurse indicated the door leading to the Intensive Care Unit.

Don was aware of low, murmured conversations from outside, breaking the silence within the room. A burst of laughter was quickly stifled. His mother's colour seemed to be worse, her face resembling parchment. Was this what dying was about? Life going on around you while you quietly slipped away. He wasn't annoyed that someone could laugh while he was enduring such anguish, merely noting it. Then he was angry at himself for noticing these things. How could he be the detached writer at a time like this? His mother was dying for Heaven's sake! He squeezed her hand.

He thought about praying. He wasn't a particularly religious guy. Wondered if God got pissed-off with people who ignored His presence until they were really desperate. Anyway, he didn't know what to pray for. According to Doctor Rogers, the brain scans showed massive hæmorrhages. To pray for his mother's survival would be sheer selfishness on his part. To have her there, at any price, didn't seem fair. Myra Creighton had always been a fiercely independent woman. She would hate to be massively disabled, totally reliant on others. Feeling he had to do something, he prayed for what his mother would want. He was still sitting there, holding his mother's hand when Kay slipped into the room. He didn't look up as she approached.

'Don.' She spoke softly.

He looked up now, his face stricken.

'Would you get the Doctor? I think she's gone.'

Chapter five

It was a charming house. One of the more modest in Westbrook, but still pretty impressive. Don's parents had almost turned it down when they heard the smooth-tongued realtor's words as he showed them round.

'You won't get a better area. Very exclusive. Only time you see a black guy, he's cutting the grass.'

They had bought the house, because Myra loved its view of the sea, but only after Joe reported the guy to his Head Office.

Don had been awake since 5am, tossing about in his old room. When he and Kay had visited Joe and Myra they were allocated different bedrooms, even though his parents knew they lived together. Out of deference to their memory and without discussing it, they'd adopted the same arrangements last night.

It was now nine o'clock. Three hours till the funeral service. Feeling he had to keep busy, Don went into the study and sat down at the solid mahogany desk, with the vague intention of putting his father's papers in order. There was a familiar smell. Even although his Dad had given up his occasional treat of a Cuban cigar months before, on Doctor's orders, the distinctive aroma lingered on. It seemed to seep out of the leather chair on which Don was seated. A silver framed photograph of his younger self, in his graduation robes, with his beaming, proud parents, sat on the mantelpiece. He wondered idly if his father's smile hid a secret disappointment. He knew Joe had different ambitions for him. He'd taken Don to meet his friends in their workplace. Successful lawyers like John Seager, with his highly lucrative practice, brought him into his office on a work experience basis. Don knew the law wasn't for him, nor did he want accountancy, despite, in his youthfulness, being impressed by Paul Veitch's Ferrari and sharp designer suits.

'Journalism?' Don remembered the disappointment in his

father's voice, despite Joe's attempt at hiding it.

'I really want to be a writer, Dad, but I have to earn a living until I find something I want to write about.'

'You have such terrific grades. Your teachers feel you can pick and choose.'

But Don had chosen. As soon as Joe realised that he was not to be dissuaded, he backed his son a hundred per cent, despite his own misgivings.

Outside, on the beautifully manicured lawn, Trixie, his mother's white Scotch Terrier, was making a bolt for freedom. She squeezed through the gap in the French windows and padded up to the desk where Don sat, a million miles away. Her plaintive whine alerted him to her presence. He picked her up and fondled her neck.

'Trixie!' Kay, her face flushed from running, appeared through the patio door. 'I think you're really a greyhound!'

'She give you the slip?'

'Took her lead off on the beach and she shot off like a bullet.'

'She keeps looking for Mom.'

Kay could hear the emotion in his voice, despite his efforts to control it. She approached the desk, slipped her arms round Don's neck and put her face close to his.

'Why don't you leave all that right now?'

'Just had to be doing something.'

Kay picked up a scrapbook from the desk and started thumbing through it. It contained Don's interviews with Arts celebrities, Streep, Spielberg, Pacino and many others. A window in the text stated 'by our Arts Correspondent, Don Creighton.' It contained a small head shot of Don.

'I didn't know they'd been keeping those', he said.

That moved him in a way he couldn't express.

She kissed his cheek.

'It's ten o'clock, darling. You better get ready.'

Chapter six

Kay gripped Don's hand for support as they followed the cortège to the cemetery. She had tried to fight her emotions in church. As the pastor, Mr Siegerson, rose to pay a tribute to the warm, generous couple he knew so well, unlike some deceased to whom he couldn't put a face, Kay found, amidst the gentle laughter, she couldn't stop the tears coursing down her cheeks. Don had sat there, immovable, dignified. He had refused the Doctor's offer.

'A valium would help take the edge off it.'

He didn't want the edge off it. It was the last thing he'd ever be able to do for his parents. He wanted to organise and experience these last moments, no matter how painful. As they gathered round the casket and the newly dug hole, its edges softened and sanitised by green matting, he cast a glance at Ella Jackson, his mother's best friend, who was struggling to hang on to her composure. Joe's only brother had died in infancy and Myra was an only child. So there were no other family members. It was a tribute to his parents that so many friends had come to pay their respects. The mourners stood patiently, heads bowed, temporarily ignoring the urge to wipe their brows, as perspiration trickled down their faces, the older ones glad that they were still here to experience the hot June day, despite its heat and humidity.

The Pastor's final eulogy brought hot stinging tears to the back of his eyes, which he fought back immediately. He wanted to be in control, for his parents' sake.

Despite his determination to experience everything, the reception afterwards at Ella and Bob's large, opulent house, was going past him in a blur. He spoke to people but had no memory of their conversations, apart from thanking them for coming. Suddenly, despite the air conditioning, he felt he couldn't breathe and excused himself to a large, florid woman, whose name he hadn't caught, but who was prattling away to him about God knows what. He looked over apologetically to Ella before stepping through the French windows and out into the shady garden. Ella didn't even notice he was no longer in the room. She was fussing around, directing everyone to second helpings of the lavish buffet which, with the help of her housekeeper, she'd laid out. She was a wonderful cook and had really excelled herself. As Kay approached, she looked up.

'How is he?'

Kay indicated, with a nod of her head. Ella looked out to the garden where Don stood, a lonely, wracked figure.

'Get him to eat something. He's gotten so thin.'

'I'll try... and thanks Ella... for all this.'

Tears welled in Ella's eyes. 'They were our best friends... if I didn't have it to do, I'd fall apart.'

An apologetic cough behind her made Kay turn round. Harry Silverman, her editor, was standing, looking unusually awkward, not wanting to intrude on Ella's grief, but obviously anxious to be off.

'Appreciate you coming, Harry.'

He hugged her.

'Got to be heading back.'

He extended his hand to Ella.

'Nice to meet you Ella. Sorry about the circumstances.'

'Did you get something to eat?' the older woman asked anxiously.

'Don't worry. I was first in there.'

He glanced out to the garden where Don had a comforting arm round an elderly lady.

'I won't intrude, but tell Don the paper will survive without him. Same goes for you, Kay. Take a break. He's gonna need your support.'

Kay hugged him.

'Thanks for being so understanding.'

He smiled, a rare smile. 'Like to confound my reputation.'

Harry's departure seemed to be the signal people were waiting for. Nobody liked to be first. In two's and three's they left. Kay offered to help clear up, but Ella and Bob wouldn't hear of it. The housekeeper was lurking in the background, ready to swoop.

Ella put her arms round Don's shoulders. 'You go on home sweetheart. Get some rest. You look shattered. Call you tomorrow.'

Chapter seven

Of course, they weren't going home. Home was their New York apartment. Instead, they drove back to Don's parents' house. He hadn't appreciated there was so much work to do in connection with a funeral. He wasn't looking forward to going through his father's papers, but needs must. Despite the shade in which he'd parked the car, it still felt like an oven inside.

As they eased up the driveway, Don felt a sharp pang of grief as the garage door opened automatically and he saw his father's old, but beautifully shining, black Buick, parked carefully inside.

'It's in great condition, bodywork as good as new, only 90,000 miles on the clock,' Joe'd say. 'Why trade it in?'

He hadn't driven it for a while.

'My eyes aren't so good, but I like to have it, in case of emergency.'

Kay, hot and sticky in her formal funeral clothes, flapped the collar of her blouse and turned to Don.

'You ok?'

He didn't answer, but gave her hand a long squeeze.

She kissed him on the side of the cheek before opening the passenger door. 'Gonna jump in the shower.'

He handed her the house keys. She put her hand over his, sympathetically, before getting out. Don drove his car into the garage, parking alongside his father's car. He got out slowly and tried the door of the Buick. It was open. He slipped inside, onto the cool leather seats. Memories flooded back. His Dad had taught him to drive in this car. There'd been arguments, of course, fierce at times, but Joe always left him with an encouraging word. Don gripped the steering wheel, dropped his head onto it and finally gave vent to his grief.

Kay, surprised that Trixie hadn't heard the key in the lock, made her way upstairs. No doubt the dog was still in Joe and Myra's bedroom, sitting on the bed, looking forlorn. She entered the master bedroom calling her name, but she wasn't there. The room seemed strangely still. Myra's novel, her bookmark still sticking out of it, was lying on one of the bedside tables. Joe's spare reading glasses were on the other, alongside a pile of sea-going yarns, his favourite reading. He seemed to be able to read several books at once. Kay had teased him about it.

'Low boredom threshold,' was his defensive answer. As she thought about the couple, she felt their loss with the same sharp pain that had overcome her at the hospital, when she'd learned they were both dead. She had tried to put her feelings on hold, to be strong and supportive for Don's sake. Now she, too, could allow herself to grieve. She walked over to the dressing table where Myra had placed a box of fancy paper tissues. It was opened. A make-up stained tissue lay in the waste bucket below the dressing table, where Myra had left it. A faint aroma of Estée Lauder's *Knowing*, Myra's favourite perfume, hung in the air. That, too, nearly started the floodgates again, but grabbing control of herself, she hastily wiped away the tears as she crossed to the guest bedroom. She slipped off her skirt and blouse which were now sticking to her, laid them on the bed and pushed the drawer of the dressing table closed. She hadn't remembered leaving it open, but then it had been a difficult day, where she'd found herself on automatic pilot. She'd only ever been to the funeral of an aged uncle whom she barely knew, whose death had not really affected her. Joe and Myra had treated her as one of the family and in some ways she could talk more freely to Myra than she could to her own mother. God knows how Don must be feeling. A quick shower and she would go down to him. She entered the ensuite bathroom. Before removing her bra and panties, she crossed to turn on the shower. Only then did she see the movement behind the shower curtain. She smiled. 'Trixie, there you are!'

As she pulled back the curtain, a tall, wiry, Hispanic looking man, with a scar from his mouth to his left ear, leapt out at her. Kay screamed in terror. Don, in the middle of locking up the garage, heard her scream and ran to the house. Kay tried to call out, but her assailant held a knife so close against her throat that a trickle of blood seeped through.

'Shut it bitch!'

He clasped a hand over her mouth as he heard Don calling her name and quickly dragged her behind the bathroom door, pushing it to as he heard Don's footsteps on the stairs. He held her so close that his fœtid breath made her feel physically sick.

Don wondered if he'd imagined the scream. He looked in the guest room, saw her things on the bed and crossed to the bathroom.

'Kay?'

He tentatively pushed the door open. Kay's captor appeared in the doorway, holding Kay, the knife still at her throat.

'Back off,' the guy growled.

He looked wild and agitated, capable of anything.

Don came towards the man, his arms out entreating.

'Oh, God! Don't hurt her, please.'

'Get back!'

The guy lunged at Don with the knife, letting go of Kay momentarily. Don's foot came up, miraculously kicking the knife from his hand. As it flew through the air, he lunged on top of the man, grappling him to the ground. He drew back his fist, about to contact the guy's jaw. The last thing he heard was Kay's scream. 'Don!'

But it was too late. He hadn't reckoned on two of them. He merely felt the blow to the back of his head before lapsing into unconsciousness.

. . . .

He came to on the lounge sofa downstairs, gingerly rubbing an egg-sized bump, as a heavy-set looking man, with a concerned expression, leaned over him.

'You all right, sir?'

Don sat up anxiously. He could see the lights of a patrol car outside in the front garden.

'Kay?'

Kay rose from where she'd been sitting on a chair, holding a cloth to her throat.

'I'm fine.'

'You sure? You're bleeding.'

'Honest. It's just a scratch.'

The heavy set man produced his ID. 'Detective Leonard O'Malley and that's Detective Polchek.'

There was another tall and rangy looking man, in a creased suit, sitting taking notes. He looked up, nodded over.

Don swung his feet onto the floor.

'Take it easy, sir. That's a nasty bump on your head.'

'I'm ok.'

'We'll have the medic check you both out.'

O'Malley's tone didn't brook any argument.

Don rubbed his eyes wearily.

'Who were those guys?'

'Burglars!' O'Malley almost spat out the word.

'Your fiancée tells me you were attending your parents' funeral.'

Don nodded.

'It's standard m.o. They go through the newspapers looking for funeral notices. They know the house will be empty for a couple hours and...' He broke off, shrugging.

Don stood up angrily. 'Bastards!'

'My sentiments exactly,' said Polchek.

'You'd have put it stronger.' O'Malley allowed himself a half-grin.

'Not any more. My wife's started a swear box.' Polchek said

ruefully. Says I'm a bad influence on the kids.'

Don looked around. 'What about my mother's dog? She usually barks her head off at strangers.'

Polchek crossed to the door, leading to the hallway.

'Through here Mr Creighton.'

He stepped aside to let Don through. Trixie's lifeless body, her white coat suffused with blood, lay on the parquet flooring. Her constancy as a watch dog had clearly cost the little animal her life. Don sank to his knees beside her. Kay holding his shoulder, wept quietly.

Chapter eight

Ella Jackson got out of her Toyota and glanced at the patrol car outside her late friend's house. She could scarcely take in what Don had told her on the telephone. He opened the front door. Kay was behind him. She hugged them both.

'Oh honey, this is the last thing you guys need.'

'Sorry to bother you Ella, but the cops want to know what's missing. You might have a better idea.' Don attempted a half-hearted smile. 'I'm not the most observant of guys when it comes to jewellery.'

Polchek led them through to the master bedroom.

'Go ahead' he said. 'They've dusted in here.'

Don looked at him inquiringly. Polchek shrugged, 'Could bet my pay check the fingerprints won't be your intruders. Those guys were pros.'

Don opened a silver-plated jewellery box. It started to play a tinkly version of *Au Clair de la Lune*.

'I bought that for Mom. First time I went on holiday without them.'

'Switzerland,' Ella choked back her tears. 'She worried so much about you climbing mountains.'

'There was jewellery in here. Stuff that belonged to my grandmother, I think…' He broke off, struggled to contain his emotions. It was anger, in the main, that rose to the surface. To think those bastards had raked through his mother's personal possessions. Their only consideration, what they would fetch. It was like a personal attack on her memory. 'Maybe you can remember the rest, Ella.'

He quietly left the room.

Myra had a lot of jewellery. Ella could remember the main pieces. She used to tease her own husband about how romantic and generous Don's father was. Almost every anniversary was marked with a gem of some kind.

'Huh I'm lucky if I get a card!' She'd remarked on more than one occasion to Myra.

'Take your time ma'am,' said Polchek, interrupting Ella's reverie.

After a few minutes, Kay excused herself and slipped out of the room to make them all some coffee. Don wasn't in the house or garden. She knew where he'd be. As soon as she could, she left the house and headed for the beach.

He was sitting looking out over the water, his face impassive, as Kay approached.

'You ok?'

He drew on his cigarette, but said nothing.

'Talk to me.'

Nothing to talk about. They're dead. I'm to blame. End of story.'

'You're not! If the police thought that for a minute, you'd be in jail. You hadn't been drinking. You were completely exonerated.'

'That only makes me feel worse.'

'Only because you want to punish yourself.'

Don got up abruptly, walked down to the waters edge, away from her.

'Your Mom and Dad wouldn't want that.'

As if to deflect the conversation, he picked up a stone, threw it into the water and watched the splash where it landed. The slight breeze ruffled his hair, exposing the dressing put on by the paramedic.

She walked down to where he stood, took his hand, held it for a long time, before he spoke.

'At college, guys beat up on their folks all the time… How they were interfering, real mean with them… Like they were at war… I felt kinda out of it. Mom and Dad were supportive, generous… Always up front with me.'

She put her arm round him, gently.

'I know…'

He stubbed out his cigarette.

'Did Ella give the cops what they wanted?'

'Yeah, whole list of stuff. She's gone home. Says if there's anything you need, just call her.'

'Polchek?'

'He's gone too. Wants you to check your folks' passports are still there.'

He looked at her inquiringly.

'Apparently they're worth something on the black market.'

Chapter nine

He realised he'd been sitting at the desk for some time, just staring into space. Passports. Focus! He couldn't face looking for them last night. Rifling through his father's cabinets seemed like an invasion of privacy. He'd slept the sleep of total exhaustion, waking up momentarily feeling his usual cheerful self. Then it hit him. They were dead. He would never see them again. The sense of loss hit him like a blow to the stomach. He got up, went to Kay's room needing the comfort of her warm living flesh. She wasn't there. He padded downstairs in his bare feet and found her in the kitchen, busily preparing breakfast.

'Oh, I was going to bring this up to you.'

She was busy grilling bacon.

'How would you like your eggs?'

He kissed her. Held her close.

'I'm really not hungry, sweetheart.'

'You have to eat,' she looked at him worriedly. 'You hardly ate anything yesterday.'

He picked up a piece of toast. Lifted the glass of orange juice which was sitting on the tray she'd prepared.

'This'll do fine. Got to get dressed. Things to do.'

He'd felt better, ready for action after his shower. The restorative power of warm water hitting his body. Cleansed. If only guilt was so easy to wash off. He realised he was wallowing in it, just sitting at the desk immobile. He gave himself a mental shake, methodically started going through the drawers, from top to bottom. The passports weren't there. He suddenly remembered, lifted a flap on the desk, feeling the wood to where he knew there was a concealed drawer. He pulled it. Locked! He recalled, as a curious small boy, being fascinated by Dad's secret drawer. He wanted to open it, but his father, smiling, always refused.

'Is there treasure in there?'

His father never answered, but usually tried to divert his attention. He recollected, suddenly, that he didn't pursue it. His younger self, somehow, knew to leave it alone.

Don got up, crossing the study to where there was another set of drawers in a tall French bureau. He rifled through them. No luck. He felt along the high shelf above. Success!

There were two keys. He returned to the desk, selected one. There was a click as it unlocked the concealed drawer. He pulled it open and half smiled when he saw the passports. He opened them slowly, looked at his parents' photographs, refusing to give in to another wave of emotion. A solid wooden box lay at the back of the drawer. He took it out, tried unsuccessfully to open it. He selected the smaller key, turned it in the lock and raised the lid. There was an envelope inside, marked DON, in his father's firm handwriting. He opened it. There was an official looking document inside. He removed it, curiously. It was a certified copy of a birth certificate for the city of New York. As he read the following, his face changed.

Name   ...   Don Michalak.
Mother's Name   ...   Anna Michalak.
Father's Name   ...

Alongside 'Father's Name', there was a blank.

There was something else in the envelope. He shook it and a photograph fell out onto the desk. It was a photograph of his mother, or at least the woman he'd called mother. Myra was much younger, holding a tiny baby. He turned it. On the back was written DON and MYRA.

He was sitting there, stunned, when the door opened. Kay bore a tray with two mugs of coffee.

'Thought you'd be ready for this.'

She stopped dead in her tracks when she saw the expression on Don's face. 'What's wrong?'

He could hardly get the words out.

'They're not my folks,'

What?'

'I'm adopted.'

'Wha...?' She looked at him in disbelief. 'How do you know?'

He handed her the birth certificate. She looked up slowly.

'Is this definitely yours?'

'It's my date of birth. Unless they lied about that, too.'

'Why didn't they tell you?'

'That's what I intend to find out.'

Chapter ten

They could hear the sound of daytime television, as they rang the doorbell for the second time. Don was about to ring it again, but they suddenly heard footsteps on the parquet flooring. The door was thrown open by Ella. 'Oh, I said to Bob I thought I heard the front door.' She made a face. 'He has that damn TV on so loud you can hardly hear yourself think! Come in, come in,' she smiled. 'Lovely to see you.'

She ushered them through to the lounge, marching across the room to switch off a Western, in mid shoot-out. Bob turned to protest, but, seeing Don and Kay, his face broke into a smile. 'Hi folks, didn't hear you come in.'

Ella raised her eyebrows. 'Well don't just stand there, get the kids a drink.'

She plumped up the cushions on the sofa. 'Sit down, sit down.'

They both sat, but refused a drink. Ella could see there was something on Don's mind. She didn't have long to wait.

'Did you know I was adopted?'

Bob and Ella exchanged a look. There was an awkward pause, broken eventually by Bob.

'I said they should have told you.'

'How did you find out?' his wife asked, gently.

'Found my full birth certificate,' Don answered 'I only had the short one. Why didn't they tell me?'

Ella sat on the arm of the sofa and put her arm around him.

'Don, they wanted to protect you,' she said carefully.

'From what?' He looked up at her.

'Well...'

'I would have accepted it if I'd known.'

'We told them that,' said Bob 'but...' His voice tailed off.

'What?' Don couldn't hide his impatience.

Ella shrugged. 'They decided it was best you didn't know.'

'So they lied to me!'

Ella rose quickly to her friend's defence.

'Honey, you know they must have had their reasons.'

Bob added his support 'They always had your best interests at heart.'

Seeing that the couple were getting a little upset, Don tried a different tack.

'Where did they get me from?'

'We don't know,' they both chorused.

'They just appeared with you one weekend' Bob added.

'Did you ask?' Kay broke her silence.

'Sure,' answered Bob 'but all they said was, it was a private adoption.'

'I babysat… while they ran around buying a crib and diapers… all sorts of stuff.' Ella remembered.

'Seemed to happen out the blue,' Bob added.

Ella smiled. 'They were over the moon. Myra always wanted kids. They'd been to see about it. Just didn't happen.'

'How old was I?'

'A couple of weeks. Tiny little thing.' Ella replied.

'And they never said any more?' asked Kay curiously.

'No' said Bob. 'They didn't want to talk about it. As far as they were concerned, you were theirs.'

Kay looked over at Don anxiously. She sensed his frustration. She could hear it in his voice as he spoke.

'Does my mother, my birth mother's name mean anything to you? Anna Michalak.'

Ella and Bob shook their heads. They felt sympathy for Don. Wanted to help, but they'd told him as much as they knew.

Chapter eleven

Kay's lasagne was done to a turn, the cheese bubbling on top. She wasn't an accomplished cook, but could make a couple of dishes really well. Lasagne was one of them. She was about to ladle it onto a plate when Don came into the kitchen. She'd hardly seen him since they got back from the Jackson house. He'd been up in his father's office, presumably trying to find some answers.

'This is ready, Don.'

'Sorry, sweetheart. I'm not really hungry.'

She ignored him and served, two platefuls.

'You haven't eaten, today.'

She placed the plates on a table set for two. Filled two glasses with red wine. He leant against the fridge. 'There weren't any in the book.'

Kay placed a jug of iced water on the table and looked at him. 'What?'

'Michalak's.'

'It's an unusual name.'

She sat at the table, indicating that he should sit, too.

He remained standing, totally preoccupied. 'I'll try the New York directories tomorrow.'

'Online?'

'No, I'm going back to the apartment. Want to make enquiries in New York, try and find out...' he trailed off.

Kay rose, crossed over to him, touched him gently on the cheek.

'Don, this woman, your mother, might not want to be found. She might have a husband, family of her own who don't know....'

'I'm not stupid,' he interrupted, edgily. 'I realise that. She might not even be alive.'

'All I'm saying is... tread carefully.'

He shrugged.

'I'm a journalist. It's my job, finding out information.'

'This is different.' She hugged him. 'Just don't want you to get hurt.'

Chapter twelve

He had hardly said a word during the journey. Kay had decided to accompany him to New York. She might as well go back to work. She wished Don had given himself a little longer before trying to find out about his birth mother. He needed more time to grieve. Don, on the other hand, found that you could temporarily push grief aside by action. He needed that to stop the emptiness, the guilt.

She was surprised that he asked her to drive. Not that he lacked faith in her ability, but he usually preferred to be at the wheel. She wondered if the accident had made him understandably nervous.

She dropped him off outside a grey, depressing looking hospital building. He returned her kiss lightly before she drove away. It was obvious his mind was elsewhere. She looked after him, concerned.

The NY Central Hospital had seen better days. It had obviously outgrown its purpose. Several units had been added on, at different times, like tumours; their architectural styles infecting one another. Half a dozen patients, the walking wounded, were standing outside the main entrance in dressing gowns, thwarting the healing process, by drawing heavily on their cigarettes. He walked through the fug into the building and walked up to the reception area. The desk was manned or womanned, by an officious looking, middle aged, female. She ignored him and continued to write on a form. The badge on the lapel jacket of her light grey suit bore the name L. Hodge. Don waited a few moments then coughed, politely, before venturing a 'Good morning.'

The woman didn't even look up.

'Be with you in a minute.'

She picked up the form, crossed over to a youngish woman, sitting in front of a computer. Her hair was dyed blonde all around its clumped edges. The contrast with its black centre gave it a peculiar halo effect. Her sweater was a little too tight and low cut for the office,

Don noticed. Connie Diaz believed in showing off her best assets.

'Connie, we need their home Doctor's number.'

Connie's attention was elsewhere. Unfazed by Miss Hodge's critical tone, she filed a broken nail. Thirty dollars for a French manicure only yesterday and already she'd chipped one of the white tips.

'Didn't I put it in?' She looked up, caught Don's eye and smiled. She had a very wide, not unattractive mouth.

Hodge, angered by the girl's lack of concern, slammed down the form. 'No you didn't! This is the third time I've had to tell you!'

She crossed back to the window. Behind her back, Connie pulled a face, for Don's benefit.

Trying to regain her composure, Miss Hodge faced Don.

'Yes, sir?'

Don smiled, his most winning smile.

'Wonder if you can help me. Could you possibly give me the birth details of Don Creighton, born at this hospital April 5th 1988?'

Unlike its effect on Connie, Don's charm was wasted on Ms Hodge.

'I'm sorry, sir. All hospital records are confidential.'

'Sorry, I should have explained. I'm Don Creighton.'

'Do you have any ID?' Her tone was brisk.

Don reached for his wallet, pulled out his Press Card.

Hodge looked at him suspiciously.

'You're a reporter?'

'But this is personal.' Don said hastily.

'When did you say you were born?'

'1988. See, it's on this birth certificate.' He held out the certificate he'd found in his father's drawer.

Hodge ignored it. 'I'm sorry; we don't keep records that far back.'

Connie looked up quickly, frowning in disbelief. Don caught the look.

'Maybe you'd have something about Anna Michalak? She was my birth mother. She might have had more recent treatment here.'

'I'm sorry,' Mr Creighton.' Miss Hodge's tone became even more official. 'We can't help you. That's confidential information.'

Don sighed frustratedly

'I wonder if I might speak to whoever's in charge.'

'You're speaking to her,' said Hodge unsmiling, 'and I'm afraid the answer's still the same.' She went back to her file, dismissively.

Connie flashed Don a sympathetic look. He walked slowly towards the exit, was about to leave, but caught sight of a little public coffee bar, almost screened behind potted plants. He walked towards it, took a seat, as a smiling waitress appeared.

'What'll it be, sir?'

'Coffee, black, please.' From his half-hidden position behind a leafy fern, he could keep an eye on the reception area, without being seen.

He didn't have long to wait. He was only half-way through his coffee when he saw Ms Hodge gather up her purse, say something to Connie, before exiting through a door marked Administration. He quickly threw down some money and headed for the reception desk where Connie was sitting, stretching. As he reached the desk, a burly man appeared from the inner office.

'How can I help you, sir?'

'Actually wanted a word with Connie,' said Don

'Sure,' the man smiled and turned to Connie, who was already on her feet, but taking her time to come over, trying to play it cool. The burly man looked at them curiously. The young guy wasn't Connie's usual flashy type. She returned her colleague's enquiring look with a dismissive stare. He retreated to the inner office. She smiled at Don.

'How, d'you know my name?'

Don pointed to her badge.

She looked at him coyly, 'You just don't take no for an answer, do ya?'

'Oh, my reputation precedes me' said Don, in the same flirtatious tone.

Connie giggled. 'I'm sorry, can't help you either. Regulations.'

Don assumed an innocent expression. 'I haven't asked you anything, yet.'

'But I know what you're after.'

'A mind reader, too.' said Don, smiling. 'Sound like my kind of woman.'

'Why don't we discuss this over lunch?'

Connie believed in directness.

'You did it again,' said Don. 'That was my line.'

Chapter thirteen

Kay was finding it difficult to concentrate. She was sitting at her desk, merely going through the motions. Her mind was on Don. She wasn't used to his silences. Since his parents' deaths he seemed to have withdrawn into himself, so unlike his usual self. It was his openness that first attracted her. They had found themselves side by side at the buffet table during a political junket for Arnold Schwarzenegger. Don had been looking intently into a bowl of greyish flesh. Whatever it was, it had only been lightly cooked. Blood was seeping from it, unappetisingly. He'd turned to her.

'What the hell's that?'

'Haven't a clue, but a good vet could get it back on its feet.'

He'd laughed, showing even, white teeth. Very attractive, she thought. She glanced at his badge.

DON CREIGHTON - THE HERALD

'I thought I knew all the political guys on your paper, but I haven't seen you before.'

'Oh, I'm here as Arts Correspondent.'

'Arts and Schwarzenegger' Kay raised her eyebrows.

'I know,' he said, sotto voce, 'sounds like an oxymoron.'

They had sat together over lunch. He told her he was doing an article on show business people who'd gone into politics.

'Maybe people vote for the heroic roles he plays,' said Kay.

'Worse still, an indestructible robot,' grinned Don.

At the end of the rally he'd asked her out to the theatre. He could obtain freebies for Broadway shows at the drop of a hat. 'One of the few perks of the job.' That had been eighteen months ago and he still made her stomach lurch when she saw him. When he'd asked her to marry him after a year, she realised he felt the same way. He'd told her he loved her many times, but so had other guys. This time she knew it was for real. Don was honest and decent. They were soul mates, as well as lovers.

She came out of her reverie, aware that Janet MacGarritty, seated at the desk opposite, was on a charm offensive. Janet was one of her fellow reporters, late forties, a plain woman with a slightly hard-bitten manner. Charm was not a word usually applied to Janet, but from what Kay could overhear of her telephone conversation, she was laying it on thick.

'It's always a pleasure to talk to you, Senator Wesley. I'll be at your office at four. I look forward to it.'

As Janet put down the telephone, Kay drew her a wry look.

'How can you be civil to that creep?'

'Because she's a professional.'

Their editor, Harry Silverman, had appeared at Kay's elbow.

'We need that interview. Don't know what the hell you said to the Senator, but there's no way he's giving it to you.'

'I questioned his support for a reduction in Medicaid for the disabled,' Kay was defensive. 'He didn't like that, or my refusal to sleep with him.'

'He's such a sleaze ball,' said Janet.

Silverman shrugged 'Sometimes you just have to swallow your pride.'

Janet rose from her desk.

'Hope that's all he expects me to swallow.'

She picked up her purse and headed for the door.

Kay smiled. Janet was a match for a hundred Wesleys. The smile faded from her face as Harry asked about Don.

'He's back in town,' she answered, worriedly, 'but pretty stressed out.'

'The guy just needs to grieve,' said Silverman. Tell him to take as much time as he needs.'

'Getting back to work might be the best thing for him,' said Kay, thoughtfully.

Chapter fourteen

Meanwhile, the subject of their conversation was keeping his lunch date with Connie Diaz. As the waiter pulled out her chair, she glanced around, appreciatively.

'Hey, this is pretty fancy.'

She glanced down at what she was wearing, a non-descript, too-short skirt and a sweater with slight bobbling. She frowned. Hoped he hadn't noticed. She should have changed it.

'Wish I'd known. I look like a different person when I'm dressed up.'

Don smiled 'I like the one I'm with.'

The waiter interrupted discreetly.

'Drink, madam?'

'Definitely. A large beer.'

Don wasn't sure if it was the beer and the wine that loosened Connie's tongue. He suspected she could normally talk for New York State. He looked across at her, amazed at the amount of food she could pack away. She was demolishing a pile of ribs, floating in a sea of sun-dried tomato sauce. She barely paused for breath, talking as she ate, waving a rib around.

'A total creep!' Her tone was vehement. 'I paid all the bills. Put the food in his mouth. Come back from work early, he's in bed with this bimbo. In the bed I bought!'

'Too bad,' murmured Don, wishing she would lower her voice. The two businessmen at the next table were smiling to one another, obviously caught up in her story.

'I got fined five thousand dollars.' This in an aggrieved tone.

'For what?' asked Don, afraid he was losing her thread.

'I broke his jaw!' she said with a certain satisfaction.

'My mother says, Connie, when will you ever learn? Why can't you meet a regular guy?'

Don bent forward. With his starched linen napkin, he wiped the sauce splashed liberally on her chin. Connie looked deep into his blue-grey eyes.

'Maybe you're the kind of guy she has in mind.'

'You don't know me,' said Don, a little too hastily.

Connie sat back in her chair, resignedly.

'It's ok. Don't panic. I know I'm not your type.'

'Mind reading's not an exact science.' Don countered, anxious to keep on her good side. 'Sometimes gives you the wrong signals.'

'Don't bullshit me. I invented the game. All you want from me is information on your birth. Right?'

Don nodded, slightly shame-faced.

'I knew that,' Connie continued, 'but I thought – who knows? We'll eat lunch. He might be won over by my personality. I should be so lucky.'

Despite her matter-of-fact tone, there was a hint of disappointment. She glanced at her watch.

'Jeez! I better get back to work, or the Führer will be on my back all afternoon.'

She rose quickly, 'Thanks for a terrific lunch.'

'Connie?' said Don tentatively.

'Don't worry! I'll check the records. The Führer didn't tell you the whole story. The older case notes aren't on computer. They're kept in the store room. I'll check 'em out. Find out what I can.'

'I'm really grateful,' said Don, kissing her on the cheek.

She grabbed him, kissing him on the lips, and then stopped.

'Oops!'

She wiped the sauce from his mouth which she had inadvertently transferred, 'Sorry, can't take me anywhere.'

The two businessmen didn't even try to conceal their mirth.

Chapter fifteen

When she arrived back at the hospital, Connie slid in her pass card and entered by a side door into a corridor leading directly to the Records Office. She glanced around before entering a door marked PATIENT RECORDS. She scanned along the filing cabinet labels marked BIRTHS, stopped in front of one marked 1980-90 and opened the drawer. Footsteps stopped outside. In the split second before the Record room door opened, Connie had quickly shut the filing cabinet and opened one marked 'DEATHS - 1942'. Hodge headed towards her. The last person she wanted to see.

'Wondered where you'd got to!' Her tone was critical.

'Miss me?' asked Connie, all innocence.

Hodge didn't answer right away. She chose a file, stopped and turned.

'Don't be all day. We're busy. There's only Bryce and I on the desk.'

Connie Nazi-saluted her receding back, waiting till the door closed behind Hodge before opening the births file and resuming her search. She quickly looked through the M's. There were no MICHALAKS. Puzzled, she carefully looked through them again. Still nothing! She tried the names round about the M's. Don's mother's records might have been mis-filed. No luck!

'Sorry, honey, you don't exist,' she said under her breath.

She stood pondering for a moment, then crossed to the cabinets marked GENERAL.

She quickly thumbed through the records, stopped at a file named MICHALAK, ANNA.

'Bingo!' she pulled it out triumphantly; opened it excitedly. The file was empty.

There was something funny here and Connie was determined to get to the bottom of it, for Don's sake. If she was honest with herself, it wasn't exactly altruism. He was a really cute guy. His blue eyes seemed to see right into her mind, know what she was thinking. Ok, he was classy, probably out of her league, intelligence-wise, but look at Arthur Miller and Marilyn Monroe, she told herself. Physical attraction could overcome a lot of obstacles. It was certainly worth another shot. She had to find out more information, have a real purpose in contacting him again, and earn his gratitude. Who knows where that might lead? She glanced at her watch. She was a little late for work. What the hell! If she was going to incur Hodge's wrath it might as well be worth it. She left the Records Office and made her way to the staff canteen. It was thronged with doctors and nurses. She looked around, searching for Ann Reiner. She was usually here around this time. She spotted her at a table on her own, eating lunch. Connie quickly paid for a cup of coffee and crossed to her.

'Ok, if I join you, Ann?'

Staff Nurse Reiner looked up with a smile. 'Sure!'

Connie could be outrageous at times, but she always lifted your spirits. Ann could do with a laugh. She'd been on her feet all morning. Her varicose veins were throbbing. She'd already had them tied twice. Her surgeon didn't advise doing them again. He'd damaged a nerve the last time and for a while her leg sometimes gave way beneath her. The nerve damage had healed now but she wasn't prepared to risk that again. Whoever said 'life begins at fifty,' needed his head examined.

'How's Maternity?' asked Connie, ultra casually.

'Hectic.' Ann pushed her plate aside. 'They say the birth rate's falling. I sure don't see any evidence of it. Maybe I'm just slowing down.'

'Not popping 'em out at the same speed, huh?' Connie asked sympathetically.

'Some things you just can't hurry.'

'Kinda like sex,' Connie grinned.

'Tell that to my Harvey,' said Ann wryly.

Chapter sixteen

It had been a pretty fruitless day. Don envisaged that on reaching their New York apartment, he would have immediately swung into action. When he unlocked their door, he could hardly push it open. A pile of mail lay behind it. He picked up the envelopes. A few bills. All the rest were condolence cards. He put them aside, not really able to face them and made a cup of coffee. While he was drinking it, he glanced at the bills, and then started opening the cards. It was obvious he was not the only one who loved Joe and Myra Creighton. You could tell. People very often just wrote their signature, or expressed sentiments like 'thinking of you' on condolence cards, but family friends had made the effort to express just what Myra and Joe had meant to them. Some told little anecdotes which showed the couple's sense of fun, or generosity. By the time Don reached the last one, the sense of loss hit him hard. He put the cards aside, left the apartment and went for a walk, scarcely aware of where he was walking.

It was gently raining, but he didn't care. It was still warm, although the humidity had been tempered by the rainfall. He loved the area where they lived. When he and Kay decided to move in together, he'd sold his shoebox of a flat, she'd given up her rental and they bought a modest apartment in Greenwich Village. You didn't get much for your money there, but they fell in love with their cosy little brownstone in a quiet, tree-lined block, only a five minute walk from Blecker. The crowded streets, which normally delighted him with his writer's propensity for people watching, today seemed an irritant. He headed for the river, lost in his own thoughts then, on an impulse, cut down a block, exiting at Marco's restaurant. He hadn't been back there since the fatal night he'd driven his parent's home. Marco obviously knew. He put down his espresso, came towards Don and enveloped him in a hug without saying anything, before showing him to a quiet booth, bringing him a glass of wine without asking and placing a menu in front of him. Don gave it a perfunctory glance. 'Mushroom risotto,' he said. Marco patted him on the shoulder and crossed to the kitchen. Don sipped his wine, lost in his own thoughts. When his food arrived he ate it without any real enthusiasm. Coming here was a mistake, he thought. The happy images of his Father's birthday meal flashed before him. What was he trying to do? Rub salt in his own wounds? He remembered his mother's words when, as a child he'd fallen off his bike and had constantly picked at the scab, causing it to bleed. 'You want it to get better don't you? Don't keep touching it, leave it to heal.'

Now he was picking at his own mental hurt; wallowing in it even. He quickly paid the bill and left. He was lucky, he told himself. Some people lost their parents when they were still kids. He'd had his for twenty-seven years. Then he remembered. They weren't his parents. He suddenly felt a sense of anger towards them of which he was immediately ashamed. But why hadn't they told him? He was an adult after all! He had a right to know. He stopped, lit a cigarette and looked out over the river, remembering Ella and Bob's words 'They were just trying to protect you.' From what? He headed back to the apartment with a renewed sense of purpose. That's what he was going to find out.

An hour later he had searched the telephone directories, found twelve Michalak's in the New York area and was now about to call the last one. All the others had drawn a blank. He drew a line through the eleventh number on his notepad; tapped in the last number. It was in Queens. The phone barely rang before it was picked up, slightly disconcerting him.

A gruff male voice was at the other end.

'Yeah?'

'Hi, I'm sorry to bother you,' said Don. 'Do you have an Anna Michalak at that number?'

'Yeah.' The guy sounded wary.

'You do?' He sat up, suddenly tense. 'I wonder if I might have a word with her.'

'Who the hell is this?' said the man.

'The name's Creighton, Don Creighton. It's really important I speak to her ... In bed...? I see... May I ask who you are? Her father. How old is she?... Four!'

'You a friggin' pervert?' shouted the man angrily. 'I can get a trace on this line, buddy.'

'No I'm not, I can assure you. I'm just trying to find my mother. Can you tell me, are there any older Anna Michalaks in your family... someone she might have been named after?'

'No... and don't call here again!' the man bellowed. Don recoiled as the phone was slammed down.

He slowly drew a line through the last name. The door bell rang. Kay must have forgotten her key. He crossed the room, opened the front door. Connie Diaz stood there. She was much more dressed up, in a bright yellow jacket with a green and yellow frill around the collar. Her idea of class, but way off the mark.

'I know you said yesterday to call you,' said Connie, 'but I was in the neighbourhood.'

'Come in... It's... eh... good to see you.' Don was slightly taken aback.

'That was a lie,' said Connie.

'No, no,' said Don 'I mean it.'

'No, about being in the neighbourhood. Thought I'd have another crack at you. Give you the information in person.'

'You found out something?' Don could hardly contain his eagerness.

'I figured that was all you were after,' Connie found it difficult to hide her disappointment.

'I'm sorry,' said Don hastily. 'Sit down. Have a drink. Beer, right?'

'You remembered,' Connie answered, pleased.

Don brought two bottles of German beer from the refrigerator. He was about to flip the top off hers with an opener, but she took it out his hand.

'That's ok,' said Connie, opening it with her teeth.

'A girl of many talents,' smiled Don.

'You ain't seen nothing.' Her tone was heavy with innuendo.

'About that information?'

'Right!' said Connie, vehemently. 'Somethin' stinks!'

'How do you mean?'

'I have a feeling when somethin' ain't right,' Connie lowered her voice conspiratorially, 'an instinct, you might say… My mom says I get it from my Aunt Maria, back home. She reads fortunes from chicken shit.'

Don tried to hide his impatience.

'What did you find out?'

'Zilch,' said Connie. 'Nada.'

She saw the look of disappointment cross his face, but spoke on, anxious to keep his interest.

'But don't you see, honey? That ain't usual. There's absolutely nothin' about you in the birth records.'

'Are you certain?'

'Positive! You sure about your birth date?'

'Well, that's the date on my birth certificate.'

'I looked around in case it had been misfiled. I was very, very thorough' said Connie proudly.

'But no luck', said Don, dejected.

'Hang on, there's more.'

She was enjoying building up her role.

'What?'

'I was suspicious, so I checked for your mother's file.'

'Nothing?'

She shook her head 'There was a case file, sure, but the records had bin removed. All it had was her name, Anna Michalak.'

'But who would do that, remove her records?'

'Search me! Funny, huh? I made a few enquiries, casual like. You'd have been proud of me.'

'What did you find out?'

'Nobody knew anything about the missing case notes.'

'So I'm back where I started,' said Don, disappointedly.

'Not quite,' answered Connie triumphantly. 'I've got a name.'

She opened her bag, extracted a piece of paper, and passed it to Don.

'Nancy Seager,' she explained, as Don read the name. 'She was in charge of the unit on the day you were born. It's a long shot, but it's a place to start.'

'A Miami number?'

'She retired there. Give her a call. You've nothing to lose, Don.'

'Thanks, I will.'

'Did I do good?'

He suddenly saw the child in her, hungry for acknowledgment. He smiled, a genuine warm smile. 'You did brilliantly.'

She came towards him, looking into his eyes. The child had gone. It was the woman now and she wanted more than a pat on the head.

'So how about a little appreciation.' She puckered her lips. It would have been churlish not to kiss her, so he obliged, intending to make it a brief kiss. Connie had other ideas. She put her tongue in his mouth and moved it around with the expertise of a dental hygienist. Despite his best intentions, he felt a stirring. When she started to move her hand up his thigh, he pulled away abruptly.

'Heh!'

Connie jumped at his tone, spilling her beer all over his shirt.

'Sorry. Can't blame a girl for trying.'

'It's ok. Help yourself to another beer. I'll get out of this,' he indicated the wet shirt. Crossed to the bedroom.

Connie was annoyed at herself. She'd blown it, again! He was the type who liked to make the first move. Trouble was she didn't think she'd get a second opportunity. She opened the ice-box, took out a beer. Her attention was caught by a photograph of Don and a tall brunette, stuck on to the fridge door. They were in skiing outfits against the background of a snow covered mountain. They were smiling at each other, looking very happy. Just my luck! thought Connie.

The doorbell rang. She looked back at the bedroom, then, when Don didn't appear, she crossed to the front door and opened it. The brunette in the photo was standing in the hallway, carrying a brown bag stuffed full of shopping.

Connie sized her up. Annoyingly, she looked even better in the flesh.

'Oh, the girlfriend, right?'

'Wrong. The fiancée!' said Kay, taking in Don who had just come out of the bedroom, bare torsoed. She held the front door opened wide.

'I believe you were just leaving,' she said pointedly to Connie.

The latter shrugged, picked up her jacket and sailed past Kay with as much dignity as she could muster.

Kay slammed the grocery bag down on the table.

'So who the hell was that?'

'She works at the hospital. Came to give me some information.'

Kay looked pointedly at his bare torso. 'Sure that's all she was giving you?'

He thought she was joking at first, but her face was unsmiling, angry.

'Don't be crass.' Now he was annoyed. 'This is important to

me.'

'Oh, excuse me,' said Kay in a voice thick with sarcasm.

'I thought I was pretty important too.'

She slammed out the front door.

Don was about to go after her, but thought better of it. Kay occasionally had these bouts of unreasonable jealousy. When she cooled down, she normally realised her suspicions were unfounded. Don loved her. He would never be unfaithful. He knew her well enough to be sure she'd realise that when she thought it through. Allied to that, he was now annoyed. Couldn't she understand what he was going through? How important it was to know where he came from? Perhaps he was being irrational, too, he told himself. Perhaps it was the double shock of losing his parents and finding out he wasn't who he though he was. What the hell, just this once he'd leave Kay to cool her heels. He crossed to the table where he'd left the note with Nancy Seager's name, address and telephone number written on it; the one Connie had given him before her abrupt departure. He looked at it for a while, before picking up the phone and dialling the number. It rang for quite a long time. He was beginning to think there was no one in, before the telephone was picked up.

'Hello?' The voice was frail, elderly.

'Miss Seager?'

'Yes.' Despite the frailty, the voice was bright.

'I'm sorry to disturb you,' said Don, 'but I wonder if you can help me. I understand you worked at the New York Central Hospital, before you retired.'

'Who is this?' A slight wariness had crept into Miss Seager's voice.

'I'm sorry,' Don replied, hastily. 'My name's Creighton, Don Creighton... This is a little difficult... I'm trying to trace my mother... My birth mother.' The rest came out in a rush. 'You see, I've just discovered I was adopted in 1988. You were in charge of the

Maternity Unit at the time… The name I was given was Michalak, Anna Michalak.'

There was a silence at the other end of the telephone.

'Hello,' said Don 'Are you still there?'

'I'm sorry,' Miss Seager's voice sounded strained. 'You're mistaken. I never worked in the Maternity Wing at Central. Afraid I can't help you.'

He heard the click of the phone being put down.

Chapter seventeen

It had been a year since Don had been in Miami. Last time he'd been reviewing a production in nearby Coconut Grove, before the play hit Broadway. He and Kay had made a weekend of it, staying in a stylish, Art Deco hotel across the road from the beach, sitting at night in atmospheric, candlelit restaurants or on pavement cafés watching the beautiful people stroll by.

'Posers!' Kay had pronounced, derisively.

She had looked pretty beautiful herself, dressed with a simple elegance. When he'd commented, she'd laughed, her infectious laugh. 'Well if you can't beat 'em, join 'em!'

It had been a wonderful, relaxed weekend and it had been there he'd asked her to marry him.

This time it was very different. Don could feel the tension in the back of his neck as the taxi weaved through the busy traffic. The strain in Nancy Seager's voice was unmistakeable. She was hiding something. He'd booked a flight to Miami immediately after he'd put the phone down the previous night. Got himself on the earliest flight. Perhaps a face to face meeting with Ms Seager would be more fruitful.

'Fifteen dollars,' the Cuban American driver said drawing up at Seagrove, a large, white, featureless condominium, which paid no lip service to Miami's architectural heritage. He sped off, obviously in a hurry. Don stood on the sidewalk in the blazing heat, putting his change back in his wallet. A few unoccupied white chairs were placed on the immaculate lawn; their umbrellas folded in such a way that they seemed like Capuchin monks, robes gathered closely around them. Don walked up the path to the front entrance, carefully avoiding the sprinkler working overtime to maintain the greenery. He quickly cast his eyes down the names listed beside the intercom, took a deep breath and pressed the button beside the name N. SEAGER. He waited. Nothing. He waited another few minutes before trying again.

An elderly man appeared from round the back of the building. He was wearing shorts, exposing a pair of slightly bowed but otherwise sturdy legs. A gaudily coloured shirt and a brimmed hat, the kind worn in the Australian outback, but minus the corks, completed the outfit.

'Can I help you?' the old man asked, smiling.

The young guy looked ok. Respectable, he figured.

'I'm looking for Miss Seager.'

'She's round the back, son. Bit more shade round there... Barometer says it's gonna be 90 today. Too much for me. I'm goin' back to my air conditioning. Want me to give her a call?'

'That's ok,' replied Don, hastily. 'I'll surprise her.'

'Nice to get visitors,' the old man said. 'My family are in Canada. Nova Scotia. We were snow birds, came every winter. We hated the winters back home. You'll find this as you get older, son, cold gets right into your bones. So ten years ago we decided to stay, but my wife died last year. It's not the same now.'

Don tried to mutter commiserations, but the man carried on.

'Our son only comes about two weeks a year, but I look forward to it.'

'Thanks for your help,' said Don, aware of the old guy's loneliness, not wanting to be rude, but anxious not to get drawn into further conversation.

'That's it. Keep goin' to your right.' The man looked after Don's retreating figure.

The old guy was right. It was a little oasis round the back. Large palm trees filtered the worst of the sun's rays. Two elderly ladies sat there, under an umbrella, on either side of a table with a jug of iced water and two glasses. One looked as if she was half asleep. The other was reading a book. She looked up as Don approached.

'I'm looking for Miss Seager.'

'That's me.' She had bright kindly eyes.

'I'm Don Creighton. We spoke on the telephone last night.'

The old lady's face changed. She gave him a troubled look, before speaking.

'Told you. I can't help you. I'm sorry.'

'Can't or won't?'

He hadn't meant to raise his voice, but he'd wakened her companion, who looked at him, startled.

'Who are you? You selling something?'

'I've nothing to say,' said Nancy Seager, avoiding his gaze. Her voice was a little tremulous.

'You want I should get the janitor?' said her companion.

She started to rise, but Nancy put a restraining hand on her arm.

'It's ok, Mamie.'

'Please, Miss Seager,' Don pleaded. 'I've flown all the way from New York.'

Nancy looked at him for, what seemed to Don, a long time, then rose, reaching for her stick.

'You'll be needing a cup of coffee, then.'

She started to walk, with difficulty. Her left hip was obviously giving her trouble. Don hesitated for a moment, then took her arm, helping her towards the building.

Nancy's apartment was cool and welcoming after the heat and humidity. Don gratefully drank the iced water she offered, as he looked around. The strong aroma of brewing coffee wafted through from the kitchen. Lots of family photos, one of a much younger Nancy at the top of the Empire State building, with a man who bore a strong resemblance to her; brother perhaps? A small crucifix on one of the walls and a reproduction of Michelangelo's Pieta took pride of place on the dresser.

She appeared at the kitchen door. He rose to take the tray from her.

'Sure you don't want something to eat?'

'No thanks. That's kind of you.'

She poured the coffee.

'Be no bother to make a sandwich.'

'Thank you no, coffee's fine. All I need is information.'

Nancy lowered herself slowly into an armchair. If she'd heard the last bit, she ignored it, busying herself with cream and sugar.

'I didn't believe you last night, Miss Seager,' Don persisted. 'I felt you knew something.'

A flicker crossed her face. He found it difficult to read. Guarded perhaps? She turned to him, fixed him with a steady gaze.

'Don... tell me... have you had a nice life?'

'I guess so,' he answered.

'Your parents? They good to you?'

'Yes'... A rush of emotion caught his voice. 'They died recently... car crash.'

'I'm so sorry.' She reached over, patted his hand.

'They were the best,' he said hoarsely.

'Well... maybe that's...' Nancy's tone was hesitant, 'That's what you should... hang on to... those memories.'

Don looked at her.

'You do know something.'

'Why rake up the past?' She looked uneasy.

'Because... I need to know... who I am.'

She looked at him earnestly, a tear at the back of her eye.

'Promised I would never talk about it.'

'Promised who?' he asked.

She started to rise. 'Let me freshen up that coffee.'

Don put a gently restraining hand on hers.

'Miss Seager, please!'

She sat back down again. 'This isn't easy.'

There was a pause. He could see that she was debating with herself. Finally she spoke.

'I wasn't lying to you when we spoke on the telephone. I didn't work in Maternity. I was in Gynæcology.'

Don leant forward intently.

'Look, I don't know all the details,' she continued… 'all I know is… I came into the sluice room at the hospital and you were there… still alive.' She looked at him, agitated.

'I couldn't just leave you like that.'

'I don't understand,' said Don bewildered.

'I told you,' she said, upset. 'Some things are better not talked about.'

'What are you saying?' Don persisted.

'You were supposed to be dead… Your mother came in for a… late termination.'

Don could scarcely take in what he was hearing.

'You were pretty weak,' she continued in a rush, 'but you were still breathing. I didn't know what to do… Didn't want to go away. You looked so helpless… so I thought I'd stay with you… till… you passed away.'

'My God,' Don's voice was barely audible.

'I got some water and I baptised you. Named you Don, after my brother… and… I just sat talking to you, trying to comfort you.'

Don could feel tears pricking the back of his eyes. He wiped them away hastily.

'Then I realised you were putting up a fight,' Nancy gave a little smile, 'so I called the Consultant… demanded they put you in an incubator. So you've got him to thank for being here today.'

She looked at Don, worriedly. The colour had drained from his face.

'Are you ok?'

She poured him a glass of water from the jug on the table, handed it to him. 'I shouldn't have told you.'

He took a drink of water, looked up at her.

'Who was he, the Consultant?'

'Doctor Howden,' Nancy replied.

Don looked surprised.

'Mike Howden? Uncle Mike?'

'He didn't tell you any of this?'

'No… He moved away… Rhode Island… Haven't seen him for years.'

'I understand he was a great friend of your parents.'

'He was my godfather' said Don. 'So what did he…?'

'He arranged a private adoption. It was all hushed up,' explained Nancy. 'Abortion survival's a tricky area.'

'I didn't know it happened.' Don struggled to comprehend.

'Afraid so. There was a conference of abortion survivors in Canada not that long ago. Now I think they sometimes give the baby a lethal injection to its heart… so that it doesn't…' she tailed off.

'God Almighty,' Don said almost to himself.

'They asked me never to discuss the circumstances of your birth. They were trying to protect you.'

Don leant back in his chair. He had difficulty breathing.

'You sure you're all right?'

The old lady looked concerned. He nodded

'I know this must be a great shock to you, but your mother must have had a very good reason.'

He leant forward. 'What do you know about her?'

'Very little. She was kinda… private, withdrawn.'

'Did she know I was still alive after the…?' He broke off, unable to say the word.

'I guess she must have known at some point. To give permission for your adoption.'

'Don't suppose she'd be bothered.'

His voice was cold; a slight note of anger had crept in.

She hesitated, then took his hand in hers.

'You mustn't judge her, Don,' she said, gently. 'You don't know all the facts. To terminate a pregnancy can't be a decision she'd have taken lightly… I know I said a few prayers for her that night.'

Chapter eighteen

Don found Mike Howden greatly aged. Uncle Mike had always seemed bright, intelligent, with a vitality that had been cruelly taken away. He seemed to be in good hands. His daughter, Anne, and her husband Luke, appeared to genuinely relish her father staying with them, not just driven by a sense of duty. They had been delighted to see Don, if slightly puzzled by the suddenness of his visit to their Rhode Island home.

He had surprised himself at how driven he had become. After the horrifying revelations from Nancy Seager, Don felt compelled to find out more. He'd flown back to New York, hired a car at the airport and driven to Rhode Island. He'd hated being behind the wheel now; found himself breaking out in cold sweats, but was determined not to give in to his fear. He forced himself to remember why he was doing this.

His opportunity didn't arrive until dinner was almost over. Anne kept apologising, saying it was a very ordinary mid-week meal, beef stew with vegetables. She felt Don must be used to fancy New York cuisine. It was the first time Don had really eaten for ages. He even had two plates of her apple pie. When Uncle Mike suggested that he and Don take their coffee out on the deck to watch the sun going down, he quickly acquiesced, glad of the chance to broach a very painful subject.

Mike paused in the lighting of his cigar.

'So you found out? Your Mom and Dad hoped you never would.'

'Can understand why.'

Don couldn't help an edge of bitterness creeping into his voice.

The old man gave him a searching look.

'Must raise a lot of questions.'

'Yes…'

'Might be best to leave well alone.'

But Don wasn't prepared to do that.

'This woman, Anna Michalak… my mother…' He found it distasteful to use a term that suggested nurturing, care. In his bitter state, the word was anathema to him. 'Can you tell me anything about her?'

Mike slowly passed a frail old hand over his brow as if trying to extract information from a vast store that was partially closed down.

'It's so long ago… I'd even forgotten her name.'

'Was she from New York?' Don persisted.

'I'm not sure… To be honest, son, that's why the family had me move in with them. I'm getting kind of forgetful these days.'

'How was she afterwards? When she found out I was still alive.'

'Didn't say much. In shock, I guess.' The old man stopped to pick up his little grandchild, Eve, who'd come toddling through to the deck.

'How's my girl?' She hugged him.

'Oh I do remember something,' he added. 'She said she was an actress. Don't think she'd done much. At least, I'd never heard of her.'

Chapter nineteen

Don was driving, his eyes closing. A truck came towards him, looming out of the mist. There was an almighty crash. He suddenly saw a body bag being zipped up. From inside, came the disturbing sound of a crying baby. He jolted awake as a key turned and his apartment door opened. Kay looked at him lying there on the couch fully clothed. Sweating.

'Where have you been?' she asked.

'Eh… Miami… didn't you get my message?'

'Yes… but you didn't say why you were going there.'

'That woman from the hospital. It wasn't what you think. She only came to give me information.'

'I know… I was being stupid.' She sat down, hugged him.

'Then I went to see my Uncle Mike in Rhode Island.'

'Why?'

'He was my godfather. I thought he might know something.'

'Did you find out anything about your mother?'

He couldn't bring himself to say the words that Nancy Seager had used. He wanted to spare her that. 'I found out she was an actress,' was all he said.

'Well, that's a start,' Kay looked at him searchingly.

'Darling, you look exhausted.'

'I am,' he said rubbing his eyes wearily.

'Right, bed!' she ordered.

He allowed himself to be propelled towards the bedroom. He hardly remembered taking off his clothes and getting under the duvet, before he fell into a dreamless sleep.

When he awoke he thought he'd only been asleep for a few hours but realised it was next morning. He could smell bacon. Kay was obviously making breakfast. He quickly showered, dressed and joined her in the kitchen.

'I was going to do that. Should've wakened me,' he said.

'You needed the rest.' Kay poured him a cup of coffee.

She picked up a note, handed it to him.

'Here. I made enquiries. Talked to Anna Michalak's agent. Anna's in New York, rehearsing at this address. That's the phone number.'

He quickly rose, grabbed his jacket.

'You've got to eat something,' she chided.

He grabbed one of the glasses of orange juice she'd poured and drained it.

'Love you,' he said, kissing her.

As he made for the door he was already calling the theatre number.

Chapter twenty

Well, Anna Michalak isn't exactly a top liner, thought Don as he alighted from the cab outside a little studio theatre on upper West Side. True, sometimes plays had a pre Broadway try-out here, but from the look of the brightly coloured poster for *Mike and the Magic Carrot*, this one was a very unlikely candidate. Children's theatre tended to attract younger actors, mainly for the sheer physicality and energy required. Judging from his birth date, his mother must be around 50, he reckoned, give or take a year or two. He remembered what his Uncle Mike had said. He'd never heard of her. Don was a frequent theatre-goer too, by the very nature of his job and the name was unfamiliar to him. Sounds as if Anna Michalak had never really made it in the business and was grateful for any paid work. He took a deep breath and went inside.

The outer door led past a tiny, unattended box office to another door. He could hear the sound of a rehearsal in progress, so opened the inner door very gently. A line of actors, costumed as dancing vegetables, were onstage, in mid-routine. They seemed, to Don's professional eye, to be completely out of sync. Two guys sat in the front row, notebooks in their hands, watching them. The bearded one stood up and signalled to the keyboard player.

'Hold it! Hold it.'

The dancers ground to a halt.

'Look,' The bearded one, whom Don took to be the Director, walked over to the foot of the stage. 'I know this is only a tech, but if you don't start together, sound and lighting don't know where the hell they are.'

'It's the eyeholes, Rob,' said an aubergine.

'They're out of alignment. Some of us can't see properly.'

'That's right.' A female voice from inside a cauliflower added, indignantly. 'I've no idea where I'm putting my feet.'

The Director turned round. 'Where the hell's Wardrobe?'

He became suddenly aware of Don tiptoeing down the aisle.

'Sorry to interrupt,' said Don extending his hand. 'Don Creighton.'

'Oh, hi Don,' said the Director, hastily. 'I'm Rob Delmont.' He shook Don's hand vigorously. 'Heard you'd phoned. Glad our press release worked.'

'Jack!' He called to his assistant, 'Show Don along to the girls' dressing room. Anna's in there. I'll be through here in fifteen minutes, Don, if you want to interview me.'

The other guy rose, put down his clipboard and led Don through a passageway, then along a slightly musty smelling corridor. Don was feeling extremely nervous. What the hell was he going to say to her? He was pretty sure he was the last person she'd want to see. The assistant stopped in front of a dressing room door that was in dire need of a lick of paint, with the number 3 on it. Underneath were the names, J. Stein, L. Staple and A. Michalak. Don swallowed nervously. The assistant tapped the door and called out.

'Anna, Press to see you. You decent?'

Don felt as if he couldn't breathe as the door slowly opened. Anna shuffled round it. She was dressed as a sweetcorn. All that was visible were her eyes.

'Can you get this thing off me?' she called in a muffled voice.

She bent over as the Assistant started to carefully pull it off. Don felt edgy. It wasn't exactly how he'd imagined the reunion. Anna straightened up, smiling. She was young, in her twenties, black and certainly not his mother.

Chapter twenty-one

It had been a hot sticky day at work. The air-con had developed a fault. Kay had been working on an analysis of a long constitutional report and felt bleary eyed. She hoped Don had a meal ready. They had an unwritten rule. Whoever got home first, did the cooking. She'd called his cell-phone during the day to find out how he'd got on with Anna Michalak. Learnt he'd drawn a blank. He didn't seem sure how to carry on from there. They could discuss it over dinner. Work out a plan. Hopefully he'd done some shopping and had something prepared. She felt in need of a glass of chilled wine and one of his excellent pastas.

She rang the door bell. No reply. She inserted the key in the lock, opened the door and looked round in dismay. The place looked untidy. A half-filled bottle of bourbon and a brimming ash tray lay on the table. No sign of cooking. She called out his name as she put her briefcase down and threw herself into a chair. Don emerged from the bedroom, unshaven, fully clothed and rumpled.

'What time is it?' He rubbed his eyes, wearily.

'Nine o'clock.'

'Morning or night?' he asked.

Kay tried to hide her concern at the question

'Night.'

She rose and kissed him. He didn't return it with any enthusiasm. It was as if his mind was elsewhere.

'So it wasn't her?' she said.

'No...'

He crossed to the bourbon, poured a large measure. Waved the bottle at her. She shook her head. He threw back the bourbon, draining the glass and poured himself another.

'Go easy on that stuff,' Kay said.

He crossed to the bedroom with the bottle and glass. Kicked the door shut. She bit her lip, rose, tipped the ash tray into the pedal bin, hesitated for a moment, and then followed him into the bedroom.

Don was sitting on the edge of the bed, looking really washed out, clearly stressed. She'd never seen him like this before. Usually if anything was bothering him they talked it out. She crossed to the bed and sat beside him. Put her hand on his shoulder.

'What happened in Miami?' she asked gently.

He turned away from her. She couldn't see the look of pain in his eyes.

'That woman... Seager? What exactly did she say?'

He got up, walked over to the window, his back to her. She followed him over.

'Don, don't shut me out... I want to help you.'

'Who says I need help?' he said, with uncharacteristic sharpness.

'Anyone with eyes in their head. I understand why, sweetheart. You've been through so much.'

'Yeah, someone up there's got me by the balls.' He sounded bitter.

'You need to talk to someone, a professional.'

'I don't need a shrink.'

'Even the cops said you should have counselling.'

'What do they know?' Don was dismissive. 'They didn't even catch those guys.'

'So what are you going to do, sit around here and brood?' Frustration gave Kay's voice an edge.

'No, I'm not. I'm going back to work tomorrow.'

Kay was surprised, but relieved.

'Good. Sure you feel ready?'

'No, but it sure beats the hell out of brooding.'

Chapter twenty-two

A cab dropped them both off at work next morning. Don had decided to draw a line under the whole Anna Michalak thing.

He'd lain awake most of the night thinking it over.

He was pretty sure that, if he found her, he'd be inflicting old wounds on his mother. If he was honest with himself, part of him wanted to do that. He'd obviously suffered as a helpless baby. Why shouldn't she? Then reason took over. He'd survived after all. No harm done. He deliberately drove all disturbing thoughts from his mind. He needed to divert it. What better diversion than work?

It was interesting, but odd, the way in which work colleagues dealt with the loss of his parents. Some never mentioned it, for fear of upsetting him, or perhaps themselves, unsure how to express their sadness on his behalf. A number of girls in the office came up and hugged him. Guys slapped him on the back, giving his hand an embarrassed squeeze. Kay sat and watched him guardedly, knowing that it was difficult for him, admiring the way he held it together, knowing if it had been her own parents, she'd have been in pieces.

Eventually he extricated himself from the cloak of sympathy in the front office and tapped on his Editor's door. Silverman rose, with hand outstretched.

'Don, good to have you back. How are you?'

Don shrugged. Harry Silverman took in the young guy's drawn look.

'Sit down, son.'

Don drew up a chair.

'Look, there's no rush, Don. You could take another week. You've had a helluva time.'

'I want to get back to work, Harry. I need to get back.'

Silverman looked at him for a moment, then made up his mind.

'Ok… What do you know about the city of Edinburgh?'

'Capital of Scotland,' said Don. 'Beautiful city, apparently. Has a castle and an International Festival.'

'Biggest Arts Festival in the world. People come from everywhere to be part of it.' Silverman slid a Festival brochure across the table.

Don picked it up and thumbed through it.

'Sounds good. What's our angle?'

'American artistes at the Edinburgh Festival. They have a theme every year, usually related to a different country and its culture. This year it's our turn.'

He looked at Don over the top of his glasses.

'Does it interest you?'

'Very much.'

'I was hoping you'd say that,' said Silverman, walking him to the door. 'Do you good to get away.'

Chapter twenty-three

The place looked like a film set. Edinburgh Castle glowered over the city from its position high up on the crags, a watchful lookout. The strains of a tartan clad piper, playing outside Waverley station, filtered through the taxi window. Pennants fluttered in the breeze from standards set at frequent intervals along Waverley Gardens. The streets were thronged with people. A stilt walker, in clown make-up, strode along the pavement, the crowds parting to make way for him. A number of young student types, dressed to grab attention, in colourful theatrical costumes, handed out show leaflets, the whole scene reminiscent of a Breugel painting. The taxi driver suddenly stood on his brakes. Don grabbed the handle to keep himself from pitching forward.

'Sorry about that, mate,' said the driver.

Two figures, one in green, the other in red, dressed in lycra to look like the red and green men, *Cross, Don't Cross* traffic signals, walked in front of the cab. The red figure had his hand out in a *STOP* pose. Laughing pedestrians crossed in front of them.

'See this place at the Festival!' said the driver, in a thick Scottish accent. 'It's crazy!'

'Looks like fun,' said Don, laughing at the antics of the two men.

'Aye, as long as you don't have to work in it,' the driver replied wearily.

. . . .

His comfortable hotel room had a magnificent view over Edinburgh rooftops to the river Forth beyond. For the first time since his parents had died, Don was able to feel pleasure in being alive. He picked up the letter which the smiling receptionist had given him on arrival and looked at the Edinburgh post mark curiously. Who knew he was in Scotland?

He removed a gilt edged card from the envelope and read it aloud.

'*The American Consul, Mr Andrew Pelan and Mrs Constance Pelan, invite you to meet the American artistes appearing at the Edinburgh International Festival at a reception...*'

The date of the reception was tonight, he noticed; in a couple of hours. Time to unpack, shower, change. First things first. He was dying for a beer. He made his way down to the bar. About half a dozen young guys in kilts and fancy evening jackets were sitting there. They all had kind of thistle type flowers in their buttonholes, and ornate sporrans. Don was surprised. He always thought Highland dress was strictly for ceremonial occasions. He didn't expect to see young guys sporting it. He said as much to the barman, a stocky man in his early fifties, who had been bantering with the group.

'Och about twenty, thirty years ago', explained the barman, 'young fellas wouldn't have been seen deid in a kilt. If you saw somebody wearing one, you thought they were a bit eccentric. That's all changed. Now they wear it to dances, football matches, all sorts of places. This crowd' he indicated the young guys, 'are here for a wedding.'

'Is this because you've got your own Parliament now?' asked Don, curious.

'No, it happened well before that. There's a kind of national pride now. I'd wear one myself, if I didnae have this kite.' The barman slapped his well-fed belly.

'Now what will it be, sir?'

'A Bud' said Don. As the barman reached across, he changed his mind.

'Hang on; I really should try Scottish beer. What would you recommend?'

'80 Shilling's very nice', said the barman. 'It's a slightly heavy beer.'

'I'll try that. I like the name, kinda quaint.'

'Aye, it's to do with the beer strength,' said the barman, pouring the liquid into a glass. 'Hey,' he grinned 'listen to me, a fount of useless information. Hope you enjoy it, sir.'

Don took his beer over to a table and sent a text to Kay, telling her he'd arrived and wishing she was with him. He glanced at his watch, plenty time before the reception. For the first time in ages he felt truly relaxed.

Chapter twenty-four

The reception was in a large Georgian room with an ornate stuccoed ceiling. Don looked round for a familiar face. A throng of people were gathered around comedian Jackie Mason, laughing at his repartée. But it was the actress standing in the centre of the room, talking to the Consul and his wife, who really caught his attention. Madeline Whitney was a Broadway and cinema legend. She had recently won her third, well deserved Oscar. A few acolytes were in attendance, hanging on her every word. Others, Don noticed, kept looking over at her, but were too over-awed to approach. A tall, distinguished looking man detached himself from a group of young arty types and approached Don, hand outstretched.

'Hi,' the man said 'Robert Eliot, Vice Consul.'

'Don Creighton, The Herald, New York.'

'Glad you could make it, Don. Good flight?'

'Yeah, excellent... Excuse me,' said Don 'is that really Madeline Whitney over there?'

'Sure is.'

'Wow, she's terrific.'

'Wait till you see her performance at the Festival. It's mind blowing!' enthused Eliot.

'What's she in? I came kind of last minute. Didn't get fully briefed.'

'Euripides, The Bacchae,' said Eliot.

'Pretty heavy stuff.'

Not the way she played it, according to Eliot. The critics had run out of superlatives. It was transferring to London's West End, followed by a Broadway run. He advised Don to move quickly if he wanted to see the production. It was the hottest ticket in town.

'Right, thanks, will do. I love her movies,' said Don.

'Wait till you see her live.' Eliot was like a star struck teenager.

'Between ourselves, Don, Greek tragedy usually sends me to sleep, but I tell you, she's electrifying.'

A good looking girl, with purple streaks in her hair and a nose ring interrupted.

'Hope you're talking about me, Mr Eliot.'

'But of course,' smiled Eliot 'Don Creighton, Beth Lownie, Boston Physical Theatre Company.'

They shook hands. Beth read Don's badge. 'Press! I must be nice to you,' she said coyly.

Eliot excused himself and left Don with Beth, who quickly produced a theatre flyer from a voluminous bag.

'That's us. Traverse Theatre, just round from the Usher Hall and the Lyceum. Please say you'll come see our show,' she urged.

'Sure,' Don smiled 'that's why I'm here.'

'Tonight?' Ms Lownie was nothing if not persistent.

'Why not?' said Don.

He looked over at Madeline Whitney who had started shaking hands with people. Beth followed his glance.

'In the same room as Madeline Whitney! Wait till I tell my Mom.'

A tall, lanky guy with spectacles hovered just behind Beth.

'Our Director, Philip Schonfield,' said Beth.

'Hear you're with The Herald, Don.'

The lanky guy extended a thin bony hand. He had a surprisingly firm handshake.

'Don's coming to the show tonight,' Beth informed him, with a hint of triumph.

'Join us for a drink afterwards,' said Philip.

'Might just do that.' His attention was caught by Madeline Whitney who was saying her final goodbyes. As she crossed to the door, he excused himself and hurried after her.

'Miss Whitney?'

She was sweeping across the hall but turned round.

'Wonder if I might have a word,' he said, smiling.

She frowned 'It'll have to be brief. I'm due at the BBC.'

Don held out his hand. 'Don Creighton, The Herald, New York. May I drop you off there, talk on the way?'

'My driver's waiting,' she said, with more than a hint of impatience.

'Of course.' Don felt awkward, gauche. 'Could I fix up a time to interview you?' he persisted.

'I never give press interviews' she snapped. 'If you'd done your homework, you'd know that.'

The door opened. A burly African American in a dark suit appeared, 'Ready Miss Whitney?' He held the door open for her.

'Contact my agent, if you want a Press Release,' she said curtly as she swept through the door.

Don felt like a schoolboy, dismissed by the headmistress. He should have known better. Madeline Whitney did have a reputation for being abrasive with the Press.

He wandered back into the room, a trifle sheepish. Beth Lownie was there, ready to stroke his, by now, fragile ego.

'I'm having a party at my flat tonight, after the show.' She slipped a piece of paper into his pocket.

'My address,' she said, in answer to his look. 'Hope you can make it.'

'I'll do my best,' Don answered.

He took a couple of proffered canapés, said his goodbyes and made for the door. He had some serious theatre-going to fit in before Beth's show. He'd looked at the Festival programme and reckoned he could see at least four shows, if he didn't stop for lunch. He'd had a good Scots breakfast at the hotel, eggs over easy, fried bacon, not burned to a crisp the way he usually liked it, but pretty good, something called tattie scone, a kind of fried potato cake in a triangular shape. Oh - and haggis. He'd heard of the latter before, in connection with Robert Burns, the Scottish Bard. He knew they served it at Burns Suppers, because he'd had to cover one when he was a junior reporter. It seemed strange to serve it at breakfast, but what the heck, he'd eaten it. So, fuelled up, he made his way to venue 15, the Traverse Theatre in the West End of the city where a play called *Exit Iraq*, by a company from Boston, was due to start in twenty minutes. He flashed his press card and was eventually given a complimentary ticket from a harassed girl.

He was glad he'd phoned ahead. The queue was snaking out the door. Downstairs in the bar, crowds milled about, anxious not to miss any of the Festival atmosphere. There was a potent mixture in the air, of anticipation, anxiety and frustration. The enormous festival programme seemed like a giant box of chocolates. You selected what you thought was a butterscotch truffle, but it might turn out to be a marzipan whip. This didn't bother Don. An absolute bummer of a show could make good copy. *Exit Iraq* wasn't a bummer, but an earnest retread of every issue connected to the war, you'd either read about, or seen in a television documentary. The audience applauded warmly, not wanting to feel that their £14 could have been better spent on something more original. His fellow countrymen and a solo woman, all from Boston, acquitted themselves well enough in their roles. He spoke to them briefly in the bar afterwards, hoping to gain an original angle on their trip to the Festival. Like most actors after a show, however, they hadn't quite 'come down' and really only wanted to hear how good they were.

The next show was only round the corner at The Royal Lyceum, a rather more imposing building. Inside, it looked a very traditional old theatre with gold leaf much in evidence. The show however was far from traditional. *Hamlet* on stilts, a New York, Polish co-production. Don had picked it because he thought it sounded pretentious. He loved bursting the bubble of pretension. Its effectiveness, however, surprised him. The ghost of Hamlet's father looked terrifying. His stilts must have been enormous, because his head was almost in the flies. When Ophelia drowned, her stilts seemed to crumble into nothingness and the sword fights at the end were breathtaking. Don was unsure whether it gave any further insight into one of Shakespeare's most troubled characters, but it certainly was a visual marvel.

The next one, the unfortunately named *Satisfaction*, was a show with music, from a group of untalented college students from Vermont, whose folks might have thought it a rewarding experience for their kids to play to an international audience. When Don reached the venue, which seemed like a dungeon below the High Street, the show was just starting, in front of an audience of only six people. He left at the interval, along with four others. He needed a beer to wipe away the depressing feeling he got when watching talent-less people mistakenly strutting, or in this case tripping, their stuff.

The day was warm. As he sat outside an old pub in the Royal Mile, a leaflet was thrust into his hands for a comedy show. It wasn't American, but what the heck; he needed a laugh. He threw back his beer and jumped in a cab to the Gilded Balloon, a large comedy venue, where a Scottish comedian attacked everyone from George to Kate Bush and every English politician, past and present. He described himself as the first Nationalist comedian, wore a kilt and had the Saltire painted on his bare chest. His barbs hit home with the audience, many went over Don's head, but he enjoyed the good natured heckling and the ease with which the comedian handled the put downs. The guy was original and witty. Despite the language barrier, Don found himself joining in the laughter and the enthusiastic applause at the end.

A quick glance at his watch showed him that he had thirty minutes to eat and get to the venue where Boston Physical Theatre was performing. He had only time to grab a quick sandwich and coffee before jumping in a cab to the Traverse Theatre where he picked up the ticket Beth Lownie had left for him.

The show was pretty impressive. Set in an office where absolute physical mayhem breaks out, the cast were slick, acrobatic and amusing. Beth Lownie was the star, moving with a physical dexterity which took his breath away. Cast as the office mouse who, of course shows her true colours, she leapt, jumped, back-flipped and cartwheeled, using and transforming simple office props both amusingly and provocatively.

He was glad, when he met her afterwards, that his praise was absolutely genuine. All too often he had to pluck something encouraging from the air when meeting an actor fresh from performance. It was never the time for absolute honesty. Her eyes lit up when she saw him waiting in the foyer. She talked non-stop on the way to her flat, where a group of fellow thespians were already gathered in various states of inebriation. The music in the background was eclectic, everything from Pussycat Dolls and Ed Sheeran to Lewis Capaldi and Scottish Rock. The flat, once grand, was now worn and heaving with arty looking types, or people trying their best to look arty. They were dancing, drinking, standing in groups, talking animatedly, or passing round joints. A couple were making out on the sofa.

'Beer or vodka?' shouted Beth, above the din.

'Ok,' said Don.

'Which?'

'Doesn't matter.'

She poured him a large slug of vodka which immediately hit the spot. A slow, sexy number started playing. He didn't recognise the singer. Beth took his glass from him.

'They're playing our tune.'

They shuffled round the floor between the bodies. Beth pulled herself close. A razor blade couldn't separate them. When the music finished Don prized himself free.

'I have to get a refill.'

This time it was their Director, Philip, who poured an equally generous amount into his glass.

'You really liked the show, I hear.'

'Which one?' said Don. 'Saw five today.'

When he saw the guy's face change, he quickly added 'Only joking. Yours was terrific, congratulations!'

Philip looked relieved. 'We getting a good review then?'

'Not doing reviews here, just features.'

'Then for Heaven's sake, feature us!' Philip's voice took on an urgency. 'We need the funding.'

By the end of the night, Don was smashed. If there had been food at the party, it might have helped, but the bowls of potato chips had been demolished by the time he'd got there. He needed a cigarette. He weaved his way through the thinning throng to the bedroom where he'd left his jacket. He went through the pockets trying to find his cigarettes. The door opened. Beth came in.

'Oh, here you are.'

She started to kiss him, pushing her tongue into his mouth. Her tongue muscles seemed to be as toned as the rest of her, judging from the acrobatics she was performing. She started to manoeuvre him towards the bed. He was too drunk to resist. They fell backwards onto the bed. She unzipped his fly; suddenly realising he was out cold.

'Shit!'

Don didn't hear her. He was already in a deep troubled sleep. The dream was the one that kept haunting him. A re-run of the crash. His mother trapped in the wreckage. His father's smashed watch on the highway. The crying of a baby coming from the zipped up body bag.

He sat bolt upright, sweating, fighting for breath. He was suddenly aware of Beth waking up beside him.

'You ok?'

Despite being only half awake, there was genuine concern in her voice. The guy was looking weird, as if he'd seen a ghost. Don got up hastily, pulling on his jacket.

'Don't go.' she patted the bed seductively. 'C'mon. I guarantee this time you won't pass out on me.'

Don crossed to the door.

'Sorry.'

'What's your problem?'

She was left talking to the air, as he'd gone, shutting the door quietly behind him. She got up, annoyed. The door re-opened. Her hopes rose for a moment. Perhaps he'd changed his mind? Philip peered round the door.

'Was that lover boy, just left?'

She nodded nonchalantly, as if it was of little interest to her.

'Did you screw him?'

'Wasn't interested,' she shrugged, 'probably gay.'

'Now she tells me' said Philip, regretfully.

Don decided to walk back to his hotel to clear his head.

. . . .

The city took on a different atmosphere at night. By day he'd noticed the bright bunting, the mass of human flesh intent on enjoying itself. There were still revellers about, but they seemed to disappear into the shadows. He was much more aware of the antiquity of the place, the old buildings sinking back on their haunches, half hidden by the murk. He crossed the cobbles of the Royal Mile through one of the many traditional wynds and hurried down a flight of steps in a narrow, dimly lit, old alleyway. The antique lamps cast eerie shadows on the ancient buildings. He reached the bottom of the first flight. A sheet of flame shot out in front of him. He jumped back in alarm. A fire-eater stepped out of the shadows. A bunch of drunken revellers spilled out of an old bothy type pub, throwing money into the fire-eater's box, jostling Don in the process, spinning him round. As he turned back he was faced with a terrifying figure in an African death mask, waving a club. He pushed past and hurried on down the steps, a sense of claustrophobic menace overcoming him.

Chapter twenty-five

He decided to bypass the hotel dining room in the morning. The smell of cooking was overpowering. Instead, he sat down in the café bar area and ordered strong black coffee. The waitress was the motherly type.

'No' wanting a wee bit toast?' she enquired.

'Feeling a bit rough. Too much on an empty stomach last night,' said Don.

'Well, you're better to put somethin' in your stomach. I'll bring you some toast.'

Her tone brooked no argument. She'd probably smack him if he didn't eat something. All he really wanted was a quick coffee and lots of fresh air. The thought of sitting in stuffy little venues, watching shows, didn't really appeal to him, today. He had a whole week to fit them in. He felt like playing hookey. There was an enormous wooden map on the wall, to the left of where he was sitting. He got up and looked closer. There appeared to be a number of little seaside resorts within easy distance of Edinburgh. One in particular caught his eye - Portobello. He liked the Italianate sound of it.

'Let that toast cool a bit before you eat it. Easier on the stomach.'

His earth mother had returned with a tray bearing a cafetière of coffee, some white and some brown toast, marmalade and butter.

'Thank you.' He sat back down at the table as she pushed down the plunger and poured his coffee.

'What's Portobello like?' he asked.

He rolled the name round his mouth, giving it an exotic pronunciation.

'Ok,' she shrugged. 'No' exactly Sorrento.' She put the rack of toast in front of him.

'I'm a North Berwick person, myself. It's a lovely wee resort.'

'Far from here?'

'Not at all. Half an hour on the train.'

She turned back at the door. 'Be sure and eat something, mind.'

He forced down a piece of toast to please her. The coffee was good. Hot and strong. After two cups he felt a lot better. As he walked towards Waverley station, Princes Street Gardens was packed with people enjoying the sunshine. The usual crowd of street theatre performers were offering tantalising glimpses of their shows in an effort to pull in the crowds. He'd found out at the party that, on average, the more obscure fringe venues only attracted an audience of six people. The cognoscenti tended to go to the main venues, as he had last night. He found more than a little desperation in the student types from all over the world, who thrust flyers into his hand. One boisterous Australian group proclaimed it was performing its show in a mini. Where the audience went, God knows! Don was glad when he escaped the throng for the relative peace of the railway compartment and the train gathered speed, past the Castle and out of Edinburgh.

Forty minutes later he was standing on soft, white sand, gazing beyond the Firth of Forth to the North Sea. It was a perfect day. Only a few wisps of cloud, the faintest tip of the brush broke up the blue canvas above him. The beach was surprisingly empty for the height of summer. True, he'd skirted the golf course to get here, not followed the signs for the harbour and main beach, anxious for a bit of tranquillity. His head was clearing remarkably quickly.

He walked along the water's edge filling his lungs with the fresh sea air, stopping occasionally to pick up a shell, relishing the isolation.

He felt unjustifiably aggrieved when he suddenly saw a female figure, in a hooded tracksuit, jogging along the path above the beach, spoiling his solitude; even more so when she started running down the slope onto the beach, ahead of him. She suddenly stumbled; her foot caught in the long marram grass and she fell over, tumbling down the rest of the way. Don ran over quickly.

'You ok?'

The woman started to get up.

'Fine, just feel like a bit of an idiot.' The voice was faintly American.

He helped her to her feet.

'Shouldn't jog in my sunglasses.'

She took them off. He recognised her immediately. She started to walk, and then stopped, grimacing in pain.

'Maybe you shouldn't walk on it.' He helped her over to a rock, where she sat down gratefully.

'Thanks. I've just turned it. Don't think it's sprained.'

'Good.'

'You wouldn't have a cigarette?' she asked.

Don pulled out a pack. 'Help yourself.'

'Supposed to have given up,' she said, pulling a face, 'but what the hell!'

He cupped his hand round the flame of his lighter. She inhaled deeply.

'Aah bliss! Thanks.'

She looked at him curiously.

'A fellow American. What brings you to North Berwick?'

'Felt like a day at the beach. Edinburgh is pretty crowded. How about you?'

'I've rented a house here. Need to be near the sea.'

'My folks are like that' said Don. 'I was brought up by the sea.'

'Whereabouts do they live?'

Don hesitated before speaking.

'Their house is in Westbrook, Connecticut... I'm about to sell it. They... died a few weeks ago.'

'Oh I'm so sorry.'

He was glad she didn't ask any more questions. She'd obviously heard the emotion in his voice. There was a pause while they both gazed out to sea.

'What's that island?' Don, pointed to a pudding shaped rock.

'The Bass Rock.'

'Anything on it?'

'A lighthouse You can't see it from this side. Oh... and gannets, thousands of them. The island in front is Craigleith and the one to your left is Fidra, supposed to be where Robert Louis Stevenson got the idea for Treasure Island, according to my landlord.' She smiled. 'I think he works for the Tourist Board on the side.'

'Interesting.' He glanced down at her foot. 'How's the ankle?'

She flexed it, gingerly at first, but then with increasing confidence.

'It's actually feeling better. So don't let me hold you back Mr...?'

'Creighton, Don Creighton.'

She gave him a searching look. 'I thought you looked familiar. We've met, haven't we?'

'Yes, the Consul's reception.'

'You're the reporter.'

'For my sins,' said Don ruefully.

'I'm sorry I didn't recognise you sooner.'

'I guess you meet so many people.'

Madeline shook her head. 'Vanity. Been told I should wear glasses, but never do in public.'

He smiled.

'You should have reminded me,' she said.

'No way.' Don grinned. 'I gather you're not too fond of the Press.'

'I apologise if I was rude, but I only went to the Consulate on the understanding that the Press hadn't been invited.'

'Why? What have we done to you?' Don asked curiously.

'Distorted my every word. Invaded my privacy. Made my life

hell... Shall I go on?' There was real bitterness in her voice.

She stood up suddenly.

He put his hand under her elbow. 'How does it feel?'

'Not too bad, thankfully. I have a show to do.'

'Good, I had to pull so many strings to get a ticket. I'd hate it to be cancelled.'

He withdrew his hand, but started to walk back along the beach with her a little way, to make sure she was all right.

'Never heard of Doctor Theatre?' Madeline asked. 'That peculiar mixture of terror and adrenaline is a great cure-all.'

'Sounds like a good quote.'

She looked warily at him.

'Don't worry,' he said smiling, helping her up the slope, back on to the pathway. When they reached the top, she turned and looked at him, as if making up her mind.

'When are you coming to the show?'

'Tomorrow night,' he answered.

'Come backstage for a drink. Let me know what you thought of it... off the record, of course.'

'I'd like that.'

'Then that's a date, Mr Creighton.'

She shook his hand and despite her injury, quickly crossed the public path across the golf course. He looked after her, hardly able to believe his luck. Madeline Whitney, of all people! Talk about meaningful coincidence. He walked back to the town, feeling buoyed up and suddenly ravenous. He saw a sign for the Westgate Gallery and Orangery Café, advertising home-cooked food so headed in the direction of the pointing arrow.

It was a delightful, airy place, full of paintings which seemed to have captured the surrounding landscape and brought the outside inside. As he tucked into home-made carrot and coriander soup, followed by chicken and vegetable pie, with pastry so light it reminded him of his Aunt Ella's, he glanced, appreciatively, at the stunning landscapes. The view he'd admired earlier seemed to have been captured all round him in delicate watercolours, acrylics and bold turquoise oils. He bought a print to take home, to remind him of the day. On the way out, his eye was caught by a silver necklace with a beautiful blue-green pendant which reminded him of the colour of Kay's eyes. It was made by a local artist. It was expensive but he bought it, thinking of the pleasure it would give Kay and imagining it round her lovely delicate neck, lying on her beautiful soft skin. God! How he loved her!

Chapter twenty-six

Back in his hotel room he justified his day off by watching the Edinburgh Tattoo on TV. It was one of the events he was meant to cover, as some American marching bands were taking part, but it was completely sold out. He hadn't been too bothered. Military bands were not really his bag. Though it did seem pretty spectacular. The colourful uniforms from every part of the world were set against the natural theatre of Edinburgh castle. He lay back on the bed, sipping his Scotch, at peace with the world. Perhaps he should call Kay? As if by telepathy, the telephone rang. He pressed mute on the TV control and lifted the receiver, heard Kay's voice at the other end.

'I was just thinking about calling you.'

'How's Edinburgh?'

'Terrific. Been to so many shows, exhibitions, you name it... Yeah, I've OD'd on culture.'

'Sounds as if it's doing you good.'

'I've missed you. We're definitely coming back here, together.'

'I'll hold you to that.'

'Oh... bought you a little present yesterday. A kilt, a mini one... Can just see you in it.'

He hadn't been able to resist it when he saw it hanging in the window of one of the tartan shops in the Royal Mile.

She heard the suggestive note in his voice and laughed.

'Sure it wasn't a present for yourself?'

The programme on TV changed to Festival Review, which reminded him. 'Hey, guess who I met today? Madeline Whitney! ... Yeah and she didn't give me the brush off this time... No... in fact, she's invited me for drinks after the show.'

'Wow.' said Kay. 'Maybe she's after your body.'

Don smiled, 'That did cross my mind.'

'She just split up with that film composer... uhuh...That's right

… about twenty years younger than her. Very acrimonious… Splashed all over the newspapers…' She grinned. 'They say she's into young studs… You tell her you have a fiancée who bites!'

'Don't believe all you read in the newspapers. You know what these journalists are like.'

She laughed. 'Take care, love you sweetheart.'

He hung up, smiling, glanced over at the TV screen. Jackie Mason was on, doing his stand up. Don picked up the remote, turned up the sound, in time to hear the comedian's closing gag, as he wound up his routine.

The Scottish presenter was back on screen.

'Thank you, the one and only Jackie Mason!'

The audience broke into thunderous applause. Don opened the mini bar took out another Scotch and re-filled his glass.

'And now, a first for Festival Review', the announcer continued. 'A lady whose Hollywood career has earned two Oscars, Numerous Tony's and Three Baftas. The actress currently causing the critics to run out of superlatives for her performance at the Festival in Euripides's *The Bacchae*.'

Don turned round to see Madeline Whitney, every inch the Hollywood idol, sweep down the staircase.

'Ladies and gentleman,' the Presenter announced 'Madeline Whitney.'

Don sat down close to the TV as the Presenter kissed her on both cheeks.

'It's great to see you here in Scotland, Madeline. May I call you Madeline?'

The guy seemed very much in awe, perhaps wary of her prickly reputation.

'Of course.'

Madeline gave him one of her dazzling smiles.

'I understand you only agreed to come on this programme, if it was in the form of a question and answer from the audience.'

'That's right.'

'I think it's fair to say you feel, at times, you have been misrepresented by the media.'

'That's putting it mildly.' The smile had left Madeline's face. 'Don't get me wrong. It happens to most people in the public eye.'

The Presenter smiled to the audience.

'Some would say it goes with the territory.'

Don saw the glint of steel in Madeline's eyes.

'This is turning rather frighteningly into an interview,' she replied.

The Presenter gave a nervous laugh. 'I'm sorry. I don't want you walking out on me.'

'Well why don't we do what we agreed and have questions from the audience?'

That put him in his place, thought Don.

'Just what I was about to suggest.' The man smiled ingratiatingly, before the camera swung to the audience.

A large florid lady was the first to the mic. Her friend nudged her, thrilled to be on TV.

'Miss Whitney. How does it feel to be working in Scotland?'

Madeline gave the questioner a warm smile.

'Wonderful. I work mainly in Los Angeles now where there are few opportunities to play classical theatre. And to be able to work in so magnificent a city as Edinburgh is such a bonus. I keep pinching myself.'

A young geeky guy, who looked like a trainspotter, asked the next question.

'I believe you came from England originally. Whereabouts?'

'I was born in Birmingham, but my family moved around a lot. Father was always looking for better job opportunities. I eventually found my way to London, where I trained. But I've lived in the States now for over thirty years.'

Don crossed to the mini bar, put ice in his drink, still listening carefully. This was saving him research time.

A third audience member piped up.

'Is Madeline Whitney your real name?'

'No. My father was a Polish immigrant,' Madeline replied. My real name is Michalak. Anna Michalak.'

Don's glass dropped, shattering.

Chapter twenty-seven

Madeline switched off the TV in her dressing room as the half hour call came over the tannoy. She liked to concentrate on nothing but the performance ahead for that valuable thirty five minutes. She'd seen enough, anyway. Thought she'd acquitted herself well enough. Though she shouldn't have shown her annoyance at the Presenter. The public would put that down to her being a diva, which she certainly wasn't. She merely valued her privacy. The guidelines had been laid down beforehand. He was just chancing his arm.

She stood up to do her breathing and voice exercises. Many of her colleagues laughed at her maintenance of a strict routine but none of her vocal power had diminished over the years, whereas many of them had resigned themselves to TV or film as they could no longer hit the back of the theatre. The voice was an instrument like any other, she felt. If you didn't exercise the muscles, they grew flabby and weak. She swung her arms, opening up her chest, almost knocking over one of the many flower arrangements in her dressing room. The place was looking a bit like a garden centre, even though she'd given away numerous bouquets to the local hospitals and old peoples' homes. Her fans and friends were always very generous and thoughtful in their good wishes. She was grateful to them because the colour and variety of the flowers vastly improved the drabness of the room. She could hardly believe this was the number one dressing room, until she saw the cramped, faded condition of the rest. So much for the glamour of showbusiness! Theatre managements put their money out front, where it showed. Not just in Scotland but in the USA. When she thought of all the black and white films she watched on television on a Saturday afternoon, when she was a little girl, she smiled. Her father used to go to football, and then she and her mother would settle down to watching Broadway musicals. Was show business ever really like that? she wondered. People in tuxedos, invariably Fred Astaire, appearing in the most luxurious, opulent dressing rooms to whisk the ermine clad leading lady off to dinner in some fashionable night club, where everyone was on their feet, applauding their entrance. There was usually a uniformed maid thrown in too, who hung up the leading lady's costume, catered for her every need and announced visitors to the inner sanctum. No, one certainly didn't do theatre now for the glamour. It did keep you on your toes, though and she relished the challenge. No retakes in live theatre. You had to get it right. She felt the churning begin in the pit of her stomach. Once she got onstage she was fine, but the adrenalin brought with it a kind of fear that she had never been able to shake off. She consoled herself that none of her friends would be out there. It was ludicrous. She could appear in a thousand seater theatre on Broadway and be relatively calm, but as soon as she knew a friend was in, she became nervous. Her friends were instructed never to tell her what night they were coming. What was that about? Fear of letting them down if she 'dried'? Damn! She did have someone in tonight. The young reporter. What was his name? Don something. She'd invited him backstage. What was she thinking about? Well, he had been so solicitous. It was quite sweet. He seemed genuinely concerned. The ankle was still giving an occasional twinge, but she knew she'd forget about that as soon as she stepped onstage. The Stage Manager announced the five minute call over the Tannoy. She wasn't on at the beginning. Time to finally touch up her makeup, but, first, the toilet. The familiar churning in the stomach could no longer be ignored.

Chapter twenty-eight

Don sat forward in his seat, listening intently, his mind in turmoil. That was his mother up there, onstage. He couldn't quite grasp the implications. He tried to stop his mind from working overtime and concentrated on the play. Madeline, playing Agave, was onstage with the actor playing her father, Cadmus. He was trying to prepare her for the sight of her dead son, addressing her with words that burned themselves into Don's very soul by their very appositeness.

'*My daughter, you and I and our whole house are crushed and broken by the anger of Dionysus. It is not for me to keep you from your son. Only I would warn you to steel your heart against a sight that must be fearful to any eyes, but most of all to a mother's.*'

As attendants appeared, carrying a covered bier, he continued.

'*Lay your burden before her, and remove the covering, that Agave may see her son.*'

The attendants laid the bier on the ground. Madeline knelt before it, her body tense. They pulled back the covering. Don caught a glimpse of a blood-stained, mutilated corpse. On sight of the body of her dead son, Madeline let out an eerie, heart rending cry, like an animal in pain. You could have heard a pin drop as she spoke, movingly.

'*O dearest child, how unnatural are these tears, that should have fallen from your eyes upon my dead face. Now I shall die with none to weep for me. I am justly punished.*'

Don suddenly had trouble breathing. He rose abruptly, pushing his way along the row, drawing disapproval from the audience members who had to rise to let him out. He seemed oblivious, just intent on getting out, fast. As he hurried up the aisle of the theatre, Madeline's lines rang in his ears.

'*I did not understand the things I ought to have understood. You, too, are punished for the same sin, and I cannot tell whether your fate or mine is the more terrible. But since you have suffered with me, you will forgive me for what I did...'*

He pushed open the theatre door and gulped in mouthfuls of fresh air. His heart was racing. He'd never felt like this before. What was happening to him? Panic attack? He wasn't subject to them, but these were pretty exceptional circumstances. With shaking fingers, he reached for a cigarette. All around him, people were pushing past, on their way to venues. Normally he would have smiled at their purposefulness. Anxious that the Festival was happening somewhere else and eager to get there lest they missed it. He seemed unaware, however, caught up in his own world. He was still standing there, a hunched figure, beads of sweat on his face as the last of the audience left. As the attendants closed the front doors, he took a final draw, stubbed out his cigarette and made his way, shakily, to the stage door, trying to compose himself. A number of Madeline's fans were standing there hoping for a glimpse of their idol. They looked at Don curiously as he announced himself and was buzzed through, wondering if he was anyone of importance. He climbed the stairs, following the doorkeeper's directions, walked along a corridor and stopped before number 1 dressing room. He hesitated and then rapped the door. The same burly black guy he saw at the Consulate, Will, opened it.

'Don Creighton. Miss Whitney's expecting me...'

He heard Madeline's voice from inside, 'Come on in, Don.'

He took a deep breath, composed himself and entered the room. Madeline was sitting there in a grey, silk, vaguely Japanese robe, a glass of red wine in her hand.

'How's the ankle?' He was surprised at how normal he managed to sound.

'Fine,' she smiled. 'Good old Doctor Theatre. Sit down, join me.'

She nodded to Will, who poured another glass and handed it to Don.

'Will, why don't you go get yourself a beer? Come back for me later.'

'Right you are, ma'am.'

Despite Will's words, Don felt a vibe from the guy. He glanced back at them before shutting the door, as if to say, 'I won't be far.'

Madeline settled back in her chair. 'Well… what did you think?'

In normal circumstances Don would have thought, typical actor, they're so insecure they just want you to tell them how good they were.

'Powerful,' he managed to say.

'They don't write them like that any more.' She sipped her wine. 'Euripides could teach some of the new guys a thing or two.'

Don didn't say anything, just looked at her steadily. 'You have a very disconcerting gaze, Mr Creighton.' Hell! She was flirting with him.

'Miss Whitney?' His voice was hesitant. 'I know you don't give interviews.'

'With very good reason.'

There was a wary note in her voice. He was past caring. He ploughed on. 'Not all newspapers operate like tabloids. There is such a thing as journalistic integrity.'

'I've yet to encounter it.'

There was no mistaking her acerbic tone.

'What if I was to let you read my copy before it was printed?'

'No' she said firmly.

'You'd have full editorial control.'

'Then I'd probably leave you with nothing to print.'

'Please let me explain,' Don persisted. 'I'm the Arts Correspondent. This would purely be about your professional approach to a role.'

'No personal stuff?'

'Absolutely not.'

'And I have a right to veto?'

'You have my complete assurance,' he said.

She thought about it for a moment, looked at him searchingly, and then seemed to make up her mind. 'When do you want to do this?'

He pulled out a note pad and pencil.

'You don't hang about, do you?' Madeline said wryly.

She took a sip of wine. 'All right. I agree.'

'Thank you.'

'Fire away.'

Don looked at her, his mind still in turmoil. He wasn't sure where he was going with this, but he wanted answers. Even if she didn't like the questions. The professional reporter side of him kicked in.

'What kind of preparation did you do for a role like Agave?'

'A lot of reading,' she answered. 'Euripides wrote something like ninety two plays. I read most of the ones that survived. Afraid they only confused me.'

'In what way?'

'Understanding their beliefs. I found it really hard to get into the skin of Agave.'

'Yet you did, very convincingly.'

'Thanks to Simon Malleson, our Director.'

'But you're the one out there, moving the audience, so you must call on your own resources. Your own emotional memory.'

'All actors do.'

'But how do you relate your experiences to ancient Greece? How do you make the text live for a contemporary audience?'

She looked at him over the rim of her glass. She liked him. He asked intelligent questions.

'You dredge... emotions, memories from your past and use them.'

'Even painful ones?' A note of intensity had crept into Don's voice.

'... Yes,' she said.

He noticed her slight hesitation before replying. He leant forward, his face inscrutable.

'The scene towards the end of the play where you're faced with the body of your son?'

'Yes?'

'You're forced to admit you've caused his death.'

'Torn him limb from limb as Euripides put it,' Madeline replied.

Don chose his words carefully. 'What kind of memories, did you ... dredge up, to achieve that... depth of despair?'

She hesitated for a moment.

'Interesting you should pick on that,' she said. 'The scene gave me nightmares.'

'Tell me about your nightmares,' Don said hoarsely.

'Well, I was terrified I was never going to make it work. First time I did it, I could see Simon thought so, too. Told me I wasn't showing the weight of sorrow.'

'Meaning?'

'Apparently, I was giving him modern angst,' she explained. 'Simon thought tears were wrong. They were not primitive. Had me lurching about the room... trying to feel this weight dragging me down...'

'That didn't work for you?'

She smiled ruefully. 'Made me feel stupid. Then he had me look at photographs of earthquake victims. Anguish on the face of survivors. You get the picture?'

Don nodded.

'None of it worked,' she continued. 'I felt lost. Actors hate that.

Emotions need to be rooted in our own experiences to find truth.'

A strained look flickered across Don's face, but Madeline, lost in her own recall, didn't notice.

'So you drew on something that happened to you?' he asked quietly. She nodded.

'Something... painful?' he persisted.

'Something I'd almost pushed from my mind.'

He looked at her with burning intensity.

She hesitated for a moment. 'I was only about... seven or eight. Had a best friend, Jim Donnelly, lived next door... Anyway, Jim was going to the Cub Scouts, and his new cap blew off into the road. He ran after it, right under the wheels of a truck. Killed outright... I didn't want to go to his house... To see him in his casket, but my parents thought I should...'

She stopped and proffered the bottle of wine. Don refused with an impatient nod, intent on her story. She re-filled her own glass and took a reflective sip before continuing.

'I remember being... frightened, but he looked ok. Just very pale. We were all standing there... the undertaker was about to close the casket when we heard this cry... I'll never forget it. Didn't sound human. More like an animal in pain... It was his mother. That's the sound I try to recreate in my performance.'

Don straightened up, his face inscrutable.

'I'm glad you found it effective,' she said, smiling. 'Are you sure you wouldn't like more wine?'

Don ignored the question. 'Was that all you used?' he asked.

'How do you mean?'

'Didn't you dredge up anything... more personal?' he persisted.

'Like what?' she asked, bemused.

'Imagine what it would be like to have a child and hold the power, here.' He grabbed her hand, holding his over it, closing her fist.

A flicker of unease passed across Madeline's face. 'What

power?'

'Life and death.'

Something in his tone bothered her. It was time to bring this interview to a close.

'Mr Creighton, I'm very tired' she said dismissively, 'I think I've given…'

'Did you ever have a child?' he interrupted.

She gave a flippant laugh, 'Me? With kids? My idea of hell. Now … If you don't mind.'

He seemed to flinch. Then came menacingly close. 'But if you had. That would be some memory.'

She didn't know where this was going, but she'd had enough.

'Look… I think you better go.'

'Some weight of sorrow, eh?' he said almost spitting out the words. He didn't seem to be hearing her. There was an odd look in his eyes. She felt suddenly scared.

'I think this interview is over.' She tried to sound firm.

'What are you afraid of?' He spoke through gritted teeth.

'It meant nothing to you? You don't even remember.' He bent over her, angrily. 'Do you?' He grabbed her by the shoulders. The look on his face terrified her. 'Do you?' he persisted.

'Will!' she cried out for her bodyguard.

At the same time, her hand reached out to grab something to protect herself. This man was obviously disturbed. She picked up her paper knife, held it towards him threateningly. Don let go his grip on her. Madeline broke away, making for the door. He followed her, not quite knowing what he was doing. She turned lunging at him with the knife. He grabbed her wrist, easily pushing her hand up and behind her head, at the same time pushing her away, in disgust. She slid slowly down the door and lay on the floor, the knife sticking out the back of her neck. Don looked at her, his surprise giving way to total panic, when he realised what had happened. He heard footsteps outside. He had to get out of there. He stepped over her body and made for the door.

As Don hurried along the corridor, Will, her bodyguard, ambled towards him.

'Interview over?' he asked.

Don, in a complete daze, ignored him, hurried past.

A look of concern passed over Will's face. He hurried to the dressing room, opened the door, feeling a sense of foreboding. Madeline was lying there in a pool of blood. He crossed over to her, bent down, felt her pulse. Her eyes were closed, but she was still breathing.

Chapter twenty-nine

Don was barely aware of his surroundings as he pushed past the fans still milling about the stage door. He made his way as quickly as he could back to the hotel, where a business function seemed to be in progress. Suited types were milling about the foyer, greeting each other heartily. He skirted around them, ignored the lift and took the stairs two at a time. He felt that he'd almost stopped breathing until he reached the sanctuary of his room. Once there, he sank down on the bed, head in hands, his mind in turmoil. What had he done? Why did he run away? The recent events, his confrontation with his mother, the stabbing, had a dream-like quality. Had they actually happened? He rose, crossed to the mini-bar and extracted a miniature brandy. Hands shaking, he poured it into a glass and threw it back quickly. The liquid hit the back of his throat with a burning intensity. He found himself gagging. He rushed to the washroom and was violently sick.

Once the contents of his stomach had emptied, his mind seemed to clear. He got up off his knees where he had been staring down the toilet bowl for the last few minutes, brushed his teeth, then washed his face and hands. There was a slight spot of blood on the cuff of his shirt. He thought briefly about changing it. Why would he do that? he asked himself. He was not going to deny what had happened. He was very ashamed of running away. What was he thinking about? It was untypical of him. He always faced up to his responsibilities. He quickly made his way downstairs. Some taxis were outside, disgorging businessmen. He climbed into one.

'Where to mate?' the driver said cheerily, delighted that he'd picked up another fare so quickly.

'The nearest police station,' Don replied.

The driver glanced at him, briefly, before moving off. The young guy had sunk back into the seat, wearily. He looked absolutely exhausted.

Chapter thirty

Kay had decided to pamper herself. It had been one of those days at the office. Frustrating, annoying and fruitless, leaving her with the need to spoil herself. She lay face down on the table, her chin resting on a rolled up soft fluffy towel, raising her up slightly, so that her boobs were not taking her weight. Gentle lulling music played quietly in the background. Where do they make these CD's? she wondered idly Is there a studio that produces music to drift gently by on? Wasn't there a danger of the musicians falling asleep, mid-performance? She hadn't heard the masseuse enter. Dana had the ability to float into a room silently. Kay felt a gentle pressure on her shoulders as Dana went to work, massaging sweet smelling oil into her taut muscles. Kay could feel them gradually relax as Dana's hands worked away on little knots of tension.

She must have nodded off as she suddenly felt Dana lifting up her hand.

'Just going to remove your engagement ring. It's so beautiful. Wouldn't want to get oil on it.'

'Thanks' muttered Kay, embarrassedly, conscious that she had been drooling.

'Have you guys set the date?'

'Not yet.' Kay didn't say anymore. She disliked conversation during a massage session. In actual fact, she and Don were about to fix a date, just before his parents' death. They'd thought of the following August, a year from now, but everything was on hold because of the accident. It seemed crass to talk marriage plans when neither of his folks would be there. They knew Don's mother would have wanted a big fancy wedding. Kay's parents back in Boston had already paid for three daughters' weddings. They might be relieved if it was a quiet affair.

She left the beauty parlour, feeling relaxed but slightly

bedraggled. A massage session always seemed to make everything, including her hair, go limp. On the way home she decided to continue being good to herself. She turned into Thassos, her favourite Greek deli. No cooking for her tonight. She hovered over the tempting display, finally settling on plump Greek olives and feta cheese in Thassos' special marinade. His wife's home made dolmades, humus, taramasalata and baklava followed into Kay's basket, along with an individual portion of moussaka and some freshly baked pita. As she was about to pay, Thassos held up a bottle of resinated Greek wine.

'You forget?'

'No,' Kay said. 'Don is in Scotland. I'm on my own tonight.'

'Oh, long way away. You miss him? Drown your sorrows,' Thassos said smiling

'No thanks. I have work to do,' she lied. She didn't like to hurt the man's feelings, but she felt resinated wine tasted like turpentine. Don liked it. Perhaps it was an acquired taste, but the bottle of Merlot, nestling in their wine rack, would do her nicely.

She let herself into the flat. It seemed so empty without him. She slipped out of her business suit into comfortable old jeans and a sweater, heated the pita bread and moussaka and laid out all the food on the coffee table in front of the TV. She poured herself a glass of wine and sat down, ready to pig out. The diet could start tomorrow. She pressed the remote and idly watched CNN news as she ate. A picture of Madeline Whitney appeared on the scene as the Newsreader read out the newsflash.

'One of America's most gifted actresses, twice Oscar winner, Madeline Whitney, is tonight fighting for her life in the Western General Hospital in Edinburgh, Scotland. Twenty-seven year old Don Creighton, a journalist from New York...'

A photograph of Don flashed on screen.

'Has been arrested in connection with what has been described as 'an unprovoked attack' on Miss Whitney. More on that later.'

Kay sat there in total disbelief, scarcely able to take in what she had just heard.

Chapter thirty-one

Don sat in his prison cell, barely aware of his surroundings. Events had passed in a kind of blur since his arrest for the attempted murder of Madeline Whitney.

Being handcuffed by police, put in some kind of holding cell, God knows where, apparently in a medical wing, lest he contemplated suicide. Aware of eyes watching him at regular intervals. The only real fact that he had taken in was that they said 'attempted.' At least she wasn't dead.

He had relived the events of that night, in constant flashbacks. When did it happen? This week? Last week? His head had throbbed constantly trying to make sense of it all. Then, just as suddenly, he seemed to switch off the tumult in his brain. Now he went through each day like an automaton and in his numb, detached state, had lost all sense of time.

He was lying back on his rock hard pillow with his eyes closed. Sleep had evaded him during the night. He felt exhausted. His cell door was suddenly unlocked, the heavy door swung open and a young prison guard stood there.

'On your feet, Creighton. You've got a visit from your brief.'

Don rose listlessly and followed the officer along a narrow drab corridor, where various iron gates were opened and relocked every few paces, before they came to a small, bleak interview room.

'Sit down, Creighton.'

Don obeyed, sitting at a table opposite a smartly dressed, distinguished looking man with dark hair, speckled with grey. The officer withdrew, remaining within vision. The distinguished looking man introduced himself as Graham Lenzie. His deep, resonant voice had only a trace of a Scottish accent. 'The Courts have appointed me to be your Defence Council.'

'I didn't ask for you.' said Don

'According to the arresting officers, you refused the services of the Duty Solicitor.'

Don looked away. He felt odd, disconnected.

'You're entitled to legal representation during your trial,' said Lenzie. 'Unless you have a serious objection, I suggest you take it.'

Don shrugged.

'Do I take that as a yes?' Lenzie asked, with a hint of impatience.

'Why not?' Don felt indifferent, as if all this had nothing to do with him.

'Good,' Lenzie opened his smart leather briefcase, extracted some papers. He eased open a button in his well-cut suit jacket. 'Now, if we could maybe just go over the events of the evening of the 22nd of August.'

Don stood up abruptly. 'Not right now.' He walked to the door dismissively.

'Mr Creighton, let me at least take a statement. It's in your own interest,' Lenzie persisted.

Don didn't seem to hear him. He approached the Prison Officer, indicating with a nod, that he wanted to go.

The officer shrugged in the direction of Lenzie and led Don away.

Chapter thirty-two

Almost ten miles away from where Don was incarcerated in his prison cell, Madeline Whitney was fighting for her life. In a large, opulent suite in Edinburgh's most expensive private hospital she lay against the crisp, white pillows, attached to heart monitors, a glucose drip feeding into her arm. A watchful nurse marked her case sheet. An eminent Physician, Sir James Perry, known to have treated Royalty, entered the room briskly and took the case sheet from the nurse. He looked at it for a few moments before coming closer to where Madeline was lying, deathly pale, her eyes closed. He bent down, close to her ear and spoke gently.

'Miss Whitney?' He waited for a moment but her face failed to register whether or not she'd heard him. He raised his voice, slightly. 'Madeline?'

Madeline's eyes fluttered open. He glanced briefly at the nurse, smiling, before turning to his patient.

'How are you feeling?'

She looked at him. Her mouth started to move, but no sound came out. He held out his hand with its neat well manicured nails in front of her.

'Squeeze my hand, if you can hear me, Miss Whitney,'

She gazed ahead, unfocussed, not moving. He put his hand in hers. 'Madeline. Can you feel my hand?'

Her eyes slowly focussed on him, as if it took a great deal of effort.

'If you do, give it a squeeze,' he persisted. He waited a few moments but received no response. 'If you understand what I'm saying, but can't move your hand, blink your eye,' he instructed. Very slowly and deliberately, Madeline blinked her right eye.

The doctor beamed. 'Excellent!' He made a note, nodded to the nurse and made for the door. The nurse bent over Madeline, checking the drip. It was then Madeline spoke, summoning all her strength. Her voice was faint, but the words were unmistakable.

'Help... me!'

Sir James turned back into the room. He'd heard.

Chapter thirty-three

Outside the hospital, a crowd of fans kept up their vigil, alongside reporters and television crews. Some had been camped outside since the star had been moved there, speculating amongst themselves as to whether she'd survive her injuries. A middle-aged woman with wispy hair and a worried expression held a sign reading **We love you Madeline**. Another sign saying **Get well soon** was waved in the air, by two female student types. The hospital doors suddenly opened and her Consultant emerged. There was a jostling for position, accompanied by cries of 'How is she?' 'Will she live?' ringing out as cameras flashed.

Sir James held up his hands for silence. A TV sound man zoomed in with a boom as the camera pointed at the doctor, who addressed the throng.

'My name is Sir James Perry, Consultant in Charge. As at eleven o'clock this morning, Miss Whitney shows a very slight improvement. She is conscious and understands what is being said to her. However, her condition continues to give cause for concern and she remains on the critical list. Thank you Ladies and Gentlemen.'

Waving aside further questions, he went back inside.

Chapter thirty-four

Don lay on his bunk staring at the ceiling. He'd just come back from exercising in the yard where he spoke to no one. A few prisoners had looked at him curiously but continued their circumnavigation. Something about him must have said 'Keep away.' He read the graffiti on the wall beside his bunk 'Piss off' it said. He found himself echoing the sentiments. That was the way he wanted it. The cell door was suddenly unlocked. Prison Officer MacIntosh, an unsmiling, tough looking individual ushered in a small cocky looking man, bearing a scar just below his eye. He walked in as if he owned the place.

'Thanks Mr MacIntosh.' His voice was thick, almost impenetrable Scots. 'Nice to see your happy smiling face again.'

'Don't worry Dougan,' MacIntosh responded grimly. 'You'll be seeing plenty of it.'

He turned his attention to Don.

'Creighton, you've got a visitor.'

Don didn't react. The guard went right up to him, holding his face a few inches from Don's.

'You deaf? Your fiancée's here.'

Don ignored him, continued to lie on the bed. MacIntosh shrugged.

'Suit yourself.'

The cell door clanged shut. The little man came towards Don, hand outstretched.

'Name's Dougan. Jimmy Dougan. How's it goin' mate?'

Don shook his hand but said nothing.

Jimmy seemed undeterred.

'Your bird's no' gonny be very chuffed.'

'Pardon me?' Don said, uncomprehending.

Jimmy grinned, 'Fuck's sake! You American?'

Don nodded. Jimmy shook his hand again.

'Oh, I love Americans. No that Judge Judy, but.'

He threw himself on the bottom bunk. 'Does ma heid in.'

Don caught about one word in three. He looked at Dougan before asking bewilderedly. 'Where you from, man?'

'Glasgow. Best city in the world.'

There was a hint of pride in the little guy's voice.

Chapter thirty-five

Kay sat in the Edinburgh airport taxi trying to think her way calmly through the steps she was about to take. Her trip, three months earlier, had been fruitless. Despite several visits to the prison, Don had steadfastly refused to see her. None of the letters she had sent to him had ever been acknowledged. He seemed to have decided to cut her out of his life. At first she'd felt disbelief, then hurt. She'd flown back to the States, her mind in turmoil. When she thought about the events, the alleged stabbing, she was in denial. At first she'd assumed it was all a case of mistaken identity. However, he'd been seen, by witnesses, leaving the crime scene immediately afterwards. Then the truth hit her. Don must obviously be suffering some kind of mental trauma. His actions were totally untypical. These people did not know that. They did not know Don as he was. He would be tried as the person they saw before them, whom they thought capable of attempted murder. She had to return to Edinburgh and convince them otherwise.

As a secretary ushered her into Graham Lenzie's legal office, the man rose to greet her, hand outstretched. He saw the strained look on the young woman's face and smiled, anxious to put her at ease.

'Graham Lenzie. Good to meet you Miss Prentice. You must have come straight from the airport. Would you like some coffee?'

Kay declined, anxious to get down to business.

'Believe this is the second time you've been over since Mr Creighton was arrested?'

'Yes, I tried to see him several times on my last trip,' Kay answered ruefully, 'but he just kept refusing.'

'Sorry to say he's the least co-operative client I've ever had' said Lenzie. 'I've been dealing with him for nearly three months and I've got absolutely nowhere.'

'This isn't like him. You've got to believe me!' Her tone was urgent, anxious. 'He's never done anything violent in his life, but he's been through so much.'

'Is that so?' Lenzie leaned forward. This case was bothering him. Perhaps now he would get somewhere.

'The trauma of his parent's accident must have triggered some kind of breakdown,' she continued in a rush. 'I've been looking up similar cases online. I even spoke to a clinical psychologist. It sounds like some kind of post traumatic stress.'

Her words tumbled out in her anxiety to convince him.

'I knew nothing of this,' said Lenzie, reaching for his notebook. 'I need you to tell me everything that's happened to him, all the details, or they're going to put him away for a long time. Fortunately for him, Madeline Whitney survived; otherwise your fiancé would be facing a murder charge.'

Chapter thirty-six

Don was stacking dishes in the prison canteen. He'd eaten nothing but an apple for lunch. He seemed to have lost his appetite and the grey, overcooked mush that passed as stew, did nothing to tempt him. Officer MacIntosh came over to him.

'Creighton. Your Legal's here.'

Don sighed, but followed him out, down a flight of stairs, through numerous gates to the Prison Hall where a weedy looking prisoner was talking to Armstrong, a fat, tough-looking individual, covered in tattoos, whom Don's cell-mate, Jimmy, had told Don to avoid. Apparently, he was trouble. Armstrong called out to Don as he passed by.

'Hey, Yankee, Doodle.' He kissed the air in Don's direction.

'Shut it, Armstrong,' Officer MacIntosh's voice had a warning note in it. Armstrong, unperturbed, grinned, but his eyes remained cold and malevolent. He was a psycho, according to Jimmy. Took a dislike to people for no reason.

MacIntosh led Don through interminable corridors till they reached the interview room where Graham Lenzie was standing, waiting to greet him.

'Sit down Don,' he said. His tone was a little warmer than it had seemed before, thought Don. Lenzie leant forward, 'I've spoken to your fiancée.'

'I didn't authorise that.' Don felt suddenly angry. Who did this guy think he was?

'Don, your trial is in two weeks,' Lenzie continued, undeterred. 'You've offered nothing in mitigation. How am I supposed to defend you?'

Don looked away. His head was hurting again. The familiar throbbing had returned to his temples.

'Miss Prentice tells me you refuse to see her,' Lenzie persisted.

'She's come over again from the States to try and help in your defence. Lucky for you she did. She told me all you've been through, your accident, your parents' death, the burglary, finding out you were adopted. She's given me something to go on. We can plead temporary insanity, have you examined by a psychiatrist...'

Don rose abruptly, toppling his chair.

'No!'

Lenzie was surprised at how aggressive the young man sounded. MacIntosh looked over at Don warningly, ready to spring into action.

'It's your only hope.' Lenzie pleaded.

'You had no right to talk to her!' Don said, fury in his voice.

'Mr Creighton, I'm on your side.' Lenzie answered gently, patiently. 'I have to offer a defence.'

'No you don't,' Don answered abruptly. 'You're fired!'

He strode over to the door. Prison Officer MacIntosh's face was impassive as he showed Don out.

Chapter thirty-seven

On the day of the trial, Don felt as if the events were happening to someone else. He sat in the van transporting him to court, feeling emotionally numb.

He hadn't slept much the night before and woke feeling irritable and jittery. That had passed, replaced by a feeling of complete detachment. He wasn't sure what was ahead of him, but he wasn't particularly caring.

Crowds were massed outside the court. Some people jeered as he was bundled out, handcuffed to a security guard. Madeline was a popular figure, rarely out of the tabloids. A battery of cameras flashed in Don's face as he was escorted into court. Someone spat at him, but missed.

As he stood in the dock between two officers, he surveyed the scene. The public gallery was packed. He saw Kay sitting there, her face white and tense. Strangely, he did not feel the surge of affection and love that he normally felt on seeing her. What was happening to him? It was the first time he'd questioned his emotions since all this started. He suddenly became aware that the bewigged Judge was addressing him.

'I understand Mr Creighton, that you are unrepresented in court.'

'I wish to conduct my own defence,' replied Don.

There was a slight murmuring in the public gallery. Kay had been utterly devastated when Lenzie had called her about this latest development. Don had absolutely no legal training. Why had he sacked his defence lawyer? She felt she no longer knew this man who was standing before her.

'That is your right,' said the judge gravely. 'I will try, wherever possible, to ensure that you understand the proceedings of this court. Before the jury is selected, I have to ask you, how do you plead?'

'Not guilty…' Don hesitated for a moment, before adding, 'Self-defence.'

There was a slight frisson in the court which ceased as the Judge continued.

'Mr Ponsonby, have you had notification of the accused's special plea?'

'No, M'Lord.' The Prosecution, a bearded man in his early forties, with the air of one who'd done all this a thousand times, answered. Don had heard from Officer MacIntosh that this guy, Ponsonby, had never lost a case. MacIntosh enjoyed telling him, but was disappointed at the lack of reaction from Don. He didn't understand the young American. He didn't seem to care what happened to him.

'Do you wish an adjournment?' the Judge asked.

Ponsonby hesitated, momentarily. 'No, M'Lord. The Prosecution is willing to proceed.'

'Very well, let us select the jury.'

The procedure passed much more quickly than usual as Don, in his detached state, objected to no-one. He suddenly became aware of the Clerk of the Court reading out the indictment.

'Donald Joseph Creighton, the charge against you is that you did on the 22nd August 2015, at The Royal Court Theatre, Edinburgh, assault Madeline Whitney, actress, cause her to be struck on the neck with a paper knife, or similar instrument, to her severe injury, permanent impairment and to the danger of her life, and did attempt to murder her.'

Don's face was impassive. Kay, in the public gallery, bit her lip.

A long list of witnesses appeared. He barely listened, until they called Madeline Whitney's physician, Sir James Perry, to the witness box. Don had not heard how she was. Only that she had survived. He supposed he was grateful for that. He leant forward.

'Sir James, on examination of Miss Whitney on her admission to the Western General Hospital, what were your findings?' asked the Judge.

'Miss Whitney had been stabbed at the back of the neck, between C4 and 5 - that is between the fourth and fifth vertebrae,' Perry replied. 'The wound had penetrated her spinal cord.'

'In your medical opinion, was her life in danger?' the Prosecution asked.

There was no hesitation in Sir James's reply. 'If she had not been found so promptly, due to the severe amount of blood loss, she may very well not have survived.'

'Were there any other marks on Miss Whitney of a defensive nature?' the Prosecution asked.

'No' said Sir James.

'No signs of a protracted struggle in which she may have raised her hands to protect herself and in so doing, received defensive injuries?' Ponsonby probed further.

'Nothing visible, no.'

'In your opinion, would this blow have come as a surprise, possibly when she had her back to the accused?' the Prosecution asked.

'Prosecution must not lead the witness.' The Judge frowned. 'Let us stick to medical fact, Mr Ponsonby.'

'I apologise M'Lord', said Ponsonby smoothly. 'As a medical expert, Sir James, what is Miss Whitney's condition at the moment?'

'She has quadriplegia. She has no sensation, or active bodily function below the neck.'

There was another murmuring in the gallery. Kay swallowed hard, looked over at Don, who remained impassive.

'And mentally?' the Prosecution continued.

'Fortunately, there is no permanent impairment in her cognitive or verbal functions. But she is mentally very depressed at the limitations of her physical state, knowing there is unlikely to be any improvement.'

'Thank you Sir James. No further questions,' Ponsonby, wound up.

'Mr Creighton, do you wish to examine the witness?' the Judge interjected.

He looked over at the young American, who seemed a million miles away. 'Mr Creighton!' He repeated his question.

'No M'Lord.' Don answered, barely audibly.

Chapter thirty-eight

He passed the rest of the morning in the same trance-like state, until a recess was called for lunch. Kay went up to the coffee bar, too upset to eat. She drank a cup of coffee, looking at her watch anxiously.

In the holding cell, Don drank the tea provided, but left the food, some kind of sausages, with lumpy looking potatoes. A Security Officer unlocked the door.

'You're on again, Creighton.'

He cast a glance at Don's untouched food.

'Should have eaten that. It's going to be a long day.'

Now it was Will Burrows, Madeline's bodyguard's turn to be questioned. The Prosecution were in full flow.

'Mr Burrows, after going to obtain your beer, did you see the accused again?' asked Ponsonby.

'Yes, sir. He was just leaving Miss Whitney's dressing room, as I came back,' replied Will.

'Did he say anything?'

'No, but he looked kinda funny.'

The Prosecution glanced at the Judge who gave him a warning look.

'Just answer the question, Mr Burrows,' Ponsonby said hastily. 'Now... when you went back into the room, immediately following the accused's departure, what did you see?'

'Miss Whitney lying on the floor, face down in a pool of blood. There was a knife sticking out her neck.'

'Label one, please. Is this the knife?'

As a clerk held up a tagged paper knife, Will nodded, 'Yes, sir.'

'Had you seen this knife before?'

'Yes, sir. Miss Whitney used it to open her fan mail. It's a paper knife. She gets hundreds of letters.'

'Where was it when you left the room, Mr Burrows?'

'On her make-up table.'

'Thank you Mr Burrows. No further questions.' Will, looking relieved, was about to step down from the witness box when the Judge interjected.

'Mr Creighton, do you wish to examine the witness?'

Don had nothing to add. The guy had been telling the truth.

'No, sir,' he said.

The Judge removed his glasses, rubbed his eyes wearily, before looking at Don steadily.

'Mr Creighton, you do appreciate that if you do not challenge any of these witnesses, you may be held to accept what they say as credible and reliable?'

'I understand,' Don replied.

Kay bit her lip in frustration. The Judge sighed.

'Very well... carry on.' He nodded to the Clerk of Court who announced

'Call Madeline Whitney.'

Now there was a decided ripple in the court. Only a muscle in Don's cheek betrayed his emotion as Madeline Whitney was pushed in by a nurse. She was in a wheelchair, her neck supported. Kay fought back mixed emotions as Madeline was sworn in. Surely Don could not have done this to her?

The Prosecutor approached the witness box.

'Are you Madeline Whitney, a citizen of the United States of America, currently a patient at The Meadows Private Hospital, Edinburgh?'

'I am.' Her voice was quiet, but firm.

'What is your occupation, Miss Whitney?'

'Actor,' she replied.

'If I may cast your mind back to the events of the 22nd August, 2015,' Ponsonby continued. 'When you finished your performance of The Bacchae that evening, you received a visitor backstage in your dressing room, at the Royal Court Theatre. Is that correct?'

There was a flicker of emotion on Madeline's face before she replied quietly, 'Yes.'

'Who was this visitor?'

'Donald Creighton.'

'Do you see Mr Creighton here in court?'

Her voice wavered slightly before she answered 'Yes.'

'Would you point him out?' the Prosecutor continued.

'I can't point,' said Madeline weakly. 'I have no movement in my arms.'

There was a sympathetic murmur in court.

'I beg your pardon, Miss Whitney.' Ponsonby was momentarily flustered.

'He's the young man in the dock.' Madeline's voice was firmer now.

'Were there any other visitors to your dressing room, on the evening of 22nd?'

'No, apart from my chauffeur/bodyguard, Will.'

'Was this your first meeting with Mr Creighton?'

'No, we met at a reception in the American Consulate, two days earlier. He asked me for an interview.'

'Which you refused?'

'Yes,' said Madeline, glancing at Don, who remained impassive.

'Did you have any other meetings with Mr Creighton prior to the events of the 22nd?'

'Yes, we met the day before, on the beach at North Berwick.'

'Was this a planned meeting?'

'No... well,' she hesitated for a moment. 'At least not on my part. I was living in a rented house there. I normally jog on the beach in the mornings.'

'You usually live in North Berwick during the Festival?'

'Yes.'

'So anyone with Mr Creighton's journalistic investigative powers might have known this and planned an 'accidental' meeting?'

'Mr Ponsonby,' The Judge intervened, 'you mustn't lead the witness.'

Kay felt a surge of gratitude towards the Judge.

'Sorry M'Lord,' Ponsonby wasn't really sorry. He'd made his point.

'Miss Whitney,' he continued 'in the past, have you been a victim of stalkers?'

'Yes, like most people in the public eye, I've had my share.'

'Have you ever had death threats?'

'Yes, unfortunately, it goes with the territory.'

'When was the last time you received a letter threatening your life?'

'About four months ago.'

'That would be just before you left the USA to work in Edinburgh?'

'Yes, I received the letter at my New York home.'

The Prosecutor turned to the Clerk of Court.

'May I have Label Number 2 please?'

The Clerk handed him a labelled letter.

'This letter has been typed on a computer,' Ponsonby continued. 'It says the words 'If I can't have you, no one else will!' Is this the letter you received at your New York home?'

'Yes. I'd received another, with a similar message, some months before.'

'Did you notify the police?'

'Yes, but they failed to find the person who was sending them. They advised me to take precautions.'

'What precautions did you take, Miss Whitney?'

'My homes in L.A. and New York are now like fortresses. And of course I have my bodyguard, Will… Mr Burrows.'

'Was your bodyguard present at this meeting with the accused in North Berwick?'

'No. Will was feeling a bit fluey. I told him to stay in bed. Somehow, I've always felt pretty safe in Scotland.'

Her eyes suddenly filled with tears.

'Are you all right Miss Whitney?' the Judge asked gently.

'Yes' Madeline said faintly.

'Would you like a drink of water?'

'No, thank you M'Lord I'm... fine.'

The Judge nodded to the Prosecution to proceed.

Ponsonby had the bit between his teeth. He turned towards the jury, but addressed Madeline.

'Miss Whitney, during your meeting on the beach at North Berwick, did you invite Mr Creighton to visit you backstage?'

'Yes. I know this was breaking my own rules, but I'd foolishly given my ankle a bit of a twist and he'd been very attentive.'

'Was there nothing in his conversation to make you wary?'

'No... not then, and I suppose, meeting him at the American Consulate gave him... a certain legitimacy.'

'To return to the night of your attack, the night of the 22nd. Would you describe the sequence of events in your own words?'

'May I have that drink of water, now?'

The Clerk of Court quickly poured a glass of water. The nurse standing behind Madeline shook her head, and then held a feeding cup to Madeline's lips.

Don, observing this, suddenly looked tense.

'Proceed in your own time, Miss Whitney,' the Judge said solicitously.

'On the night of the 22nd, I came back to my dressing room, after the performance, changed and then... started opening some of my mail... using the paper knife which a fan sent me. I stopped when Mr Creighton came backstage. Will poured us both a glass of wine and I told him to go get himself a beer.'

Kay sat on the edge of her seat, listening intently as Madeline continued.

'In the course of conversation, Mr Creighton asked if he could interview me, and I eventually agreed.'

'You were alone with him at this point?' the Prosecutor clarified.

'Oh yes, Will had only been gone five minutes. Mr Creighton started off ok, but then his questions became a little odd.'

'In what way?' the Prosecutor moved closer to her.

'He kept asking about a particular scene in the play.'

'Which particular scene?'

'When I'm faced with the body of my son, Pentheus.'

'For the benefit of the members of the jury who may not be familiar with the play, am I right in saying Pentheus has been murdered?'

'Yes, by my character, who's not really responsible for her actions at the time.'

'Would you say Mr Creighton seemed fascinated by the idea of murder?'

Kay felt very uneasy at the way this was going.

'Mr Ponsonby, I don't have to tell you this is supposition,' the Judge interjected disapprovingly. 'The jury will ignore the last remark.'

'My apologies, M'Lord'. Ponsonby switched on his penitent face.

'Miss Whitney did you become alarmed in the course of this interview?'

'Yes, I did. He, Mr Creighton, kept on and on asking me about my emotions... What I felt knowing that I'd caused the death of my son.'

'That you'd committed murder, in fact?'

'Yes.'

'And what was the culmination of the accused's fascination with murder?'

'Mr Ponsonby,' the Judge was now irate. 'I won't warn you again about putting words into the witness's mouth. That last remark will be stricken from the record.'

'My apologies, M'Lord.' Ponsonby looked suitably contrite.

He should be a bloody actor! thought Kay, angrily.

'What happened next, Miss Whitney?' Ponsonby continued, undeterred.

'It all seems a bit of a blur.' Madeline's voice became agitated. 'He was demanding to know about... the feelings I'd used to show remorse on stage, but then he reached such a frightening intensity... Gripping me so hard... Asking the same thing over and over again, that I became afraid.'

'What did you do?'

'I shouted for Will. He let me go... I started to make for the door. We struggled. Next thing I felt this terrible pain in my neck. I think I realised I'd been stabbed before I passed out.' She was now visibly distressed.

'That's all I remember, till I woke up in hospital... unable to move.'

'Thank you Miss Whitney. That will be all.' said Ponsonby.

Chapter thirty-nine

Next day, when the court recessed for lunch, Kay left the building quickly. She couldn't bear to hear the comments of the myriad fans of Madeline Whitney who'd jammed the public gallery. They were all directed malevolently at Don and were of the 'hanging is too good for him, variety'. She thanked God that there was no death penalty in Britain. Outside the court, the reporters, fans and curious onlookers who were unable to get in, kept up a vigil. Kay pushed through them and rounded a corner, anxious to distance herself.

She couldn't go too far. She only had an hour and a half. She hadn't ordered the hotel's cooked breakfast, merely settling for a yoghourt and coffee. She'd better eat something now, though she didn't really feel like it. Her mind was in turmoil. Surely to God Don would offer some kind of defence. Didn't he care what happened to him?

She entered a large welcoming restaurant, without even glancing at the menu outside. Despite its size, she was asked if she'd booked and on her negative reply, was turned away. At the small bistro next door she was again, apologetically, turned away. Edinburgh seemed to be a busy place. There was no Festival on now. Perhaps it was always busy. She crossed the road to a small coffee bar and managed to find a table. She gave a perfunctory glance at the menu, ordered a double espresso and a prawn and mayonnaise ciabatta. It came quickly. Even though it was freshly baked and delicious, she only managed half of it. Her stomach was in a knot of anxiety. She looked round at the carefree people seated at the other tables. Workmates dishing the office gossip. Girlfriends relaxing from a shopping spree. A group of students being a little too loud. She envied them all. She'd been like them not so long ago. You never know what the hell life has in store for you. She asked for the cheque. The waitress, seeing her half-eaten sandwich, asked if the food was alright. Kay assured her it was, muttered something about not being very hungry and left.

She still had half an hour to go till the court was recalled. Although it was late April, there was a strong, cool breeze blowing through the capital. Kay shivered in her thin coat. She didn't want to go back into the court amongst all that antipathy directed at Don. If only they knew what a great guy her fiancé was. How incapable he was of hurting anyone. On the other side of the Court sat an ancient grey Church, the High Kirk of St Giles, according to the sign outside. She went inside to get out of the wind chill. It was gloomy, but she found the half-light strangely comforting. Kay knelt down and prayed as she'd never done before. She wasn't particularly religious and couldn't formulate a conventional prayer. Instead, she tried to speak directly from her heart. She wasn't afraid to beg, if it would save Don

'Please God, help him. You know he's a good man. Please make sure justice prevails.'

Chapter forty

Back in court, the object of Kay's plea was in the witness box, being cross-examined by the Prosecution. Madeline Whitney, despite being pale and tired looking, appeared to be watching the proceedings very closely.

Although Kay knew Don inside out, at that particular moment, she found him very hard to read. It was as if someone had spirited away her happy, carefree fiancé and left this detached, unresponsive clone in his place.

Ponsonby approached the witness box, said nothing for a few moments, but treated Don to a searching look. This guy is pure theatre, thought Kay, angrily. This is a game to him! Eventually he spoke up.

'Mr Creighton, you have entered a special plea of self-defence. Do you still abide by that plea?'

'Yes,' said Don quietly.

'Mr Creighton, would you say you were familiar with Miss Whitney's work?' asked Ponsonby.

'Yes.'

'How familiar?'

'I've seen her movies.'

'What? All of them?' Ponsonby assumed mock astonishment.

'Most of them.'

'And how about her stage work? Have you seen any of it?

'Her Broadway performances.'

'I understand Miss Whitney has starred on Broadway at least eight times. Am I to understand you've seen all of those?'

Don shrugged. 'I guess.'

'Would you describe yourself as a fan?' Ponsonby asked with a hint of sarcasm.

'I'm an admirer of her work.'

'Would it be fair to describe you as a devoted admirer?'

'I'm an Arts Correspondent. It's part of my job,' Don replied.

The Prosecutor continued to address Don, but turned partially towards the Court.

'Mr Creighton. I understand you met Miss Whitney on the beach at North Berwick, on the 21st August, the day prior to her attack. Is that correct?'

'Yes.'

'What were you doing in North Berwick on that day?'

'I wanted some sea air. To get away from the city.'

'Why North Berwick?'

'Why not? It was convenient for Edinburgh.'

'Were you aware that Miss Whitney had rented a house there?'

'No.'

'Are you saying your meeting on the beach was pure coincidence?'

'Yes.'

The Prosecutor's tone was now incredulous.

'So of all the resorts around Edinburgh, and on a three mile stretch of beach, you just happened to be there at the same time?'

Don shrugged.'Yes.'

Ponsonby swung round towards Don dramatically,

'Mr Creighton, I put it to you, that you knew Miss Whitney was going to be jogging at that time and you engineered this meeting. Is that not correct?'

'No.'

Kay was glad to hear an emphatic note creep into Don's voice.

The Prosecutor, however, was scenting blood.

'Have you ever written to Miss Whitney?'

'No.'

'Mr Creighton, how much do you weigh?'

'About 180 pounds.'

'And Miss Whitney weighs around 110. That's a seventy pound advantage over her. Is it not?'

'Yes.'

What's he driving at? thought Kay worriedly .

'What height are you, Mr Creighton?'

'6 foot 1.'

The Prosecutor had a faint smile on his lips as he continued, relentlessly.

'Miss Whitney is around 5 foot 5. So despite a 70 pound advantage in weight, an eight inch advantage in height, not to mention the fact that you are twenty eight years her junior, you still insist on a plea of self-defence?'

'Yes.'

'Mr Creighton, you are claiming that when you came to interview Miss Whitney at the Royal Court Theatre on the night of 22nd August, she, for no reason, attacked you, and a young fit man like yourself, had to fight for his life? Do you honestly expect the jury to believe that?'

'No.'

The Judge looked up in surprise. There was a ripple in court.

'Good, now we're getting somewhere,' said the Prosecutor.

'Am I right in thinking Mr Creighton that you wish to change your story? That you now say your actions were not in self-defence?'

'I'm not saying Miss Whitney intended to kill me on the 22nd August. She didn't, but I still say my actions were in defence of my life.'

The Judge took off his glasses and looked at Don. There was a querulous, rather irritable, note in his voice.

'Mr. Creighton, I'm confused, as I'm sure the jury must be. Either your actions on the 22nd August were in self-defence, that is in response to an attack, by Miss Whitney, deemed, by you, to be endangering your life, or they were not. Which is it to be?'

'Miss Whitney did endanger my life,' Don replied. His voice was calm, controlled. 'She tried to take it from me, but not on the 22nd August.'

'Are you saying there had been a previous attack on your life from Miss Whitney?' the Prosecutor seemed genuinely surprised.

Kay, confused, looked over at Madeline, who was looking totally incredulous.

'Yes.' Don's voice was icy calm.

'Perhaps you would be good enough to tell us when and where this previous attack on your life, instigated by Miss Whitney, took place,' the Prosecutor asked.

'At The New York Central Hospital, on April 5th, 1988,' Don replied.

'Now I really am confused. Mr Creighton,' the Judge interjected.

'In 1980 you could only have been... a baby.'

'Yes. A baby unable to defend the life Miss Whitney tried to terminate.' Don's voice was quiet, but clear.

'Madeline Whitney is my mother.'

The court descended into uproar.

Chapter forty-one

Kay spent the next few days in a daze. She listened to the evidence in court which, in the main, seemed to be against Don. He was offering little in his own defence. When the prosecutor asked him if he'd gone backstage to see Madeline Whitney with murder in his heart, she couldn't believe it when he said 'perhaps', although he did add, almost as an afterthought, 'Though I don't remember it that way.'

He agreed when Ponsonby pressed him, that he was angry because his own mother had in his estimation 'tried to kill him.'

The media were having a field day debating the whole issue. Abortion survivors came onto TV chat shows to say how they'd felt on finding that they'd survived abortion attempts. Kay hadn't been aware that that this actually happened. She was a firm supporter of a Woman's Right to Choose but, she had to admit, the survival of some babies all seemed to have been hushed up. A nurse, Jill Stanek, from Oak Lawn hospital in Illinois was interviewed in the newspapers. She had apparently been asked to testify before a US House Committee for the federal Born Alive Infants Protection Act. According to her testimony, in late abortions, medication was inserted into the mother's birth canal, inducing premature labour. Some babies, in her experience only lived a few minutes, 'others survived as long as an eight hour shift. To be clear, these were living babies left out to die,' she stated. The babies were issued with birth and death certificates according to Illinois law. The Freedom of Choice Act, in the USA, however, had overruled any objections and the practice continued. Stories of back street abortionists featured largely, trying to provide balance to the fierce moral debate which Don's trial had fuelled.

The Jury members were also locked in a heated debate. They sat with empty coffee cups, trying to reach some form of consensus.

'I think he's suffered enough. You saying we should take away his freedom, too?' a motherly looking woman in her mid-fifties asked.

'We have to,' a young businessman, with a five o'clock shadow, stated bluntly. 'At the end of the day, he took the law into his own hands. You can't do that in this country.'

'He obviously wanted some kind of retribution. I think he's flipped,' this from a tall, cool looking blonde.

'Mind you,' the Chairman of the Jury, a portly, middle-aged man added reflectively 'don't know how I'd feel if I had survived an abortion. Maybe it would push me over the edge.'

Chapter forty-two

Kay had spent a sleepless night. She'd stayed in her hotel room, unable to face people. She'd ordered soup and a sandwich and barely touched either. She got out of bed at three o'clock in the morning, rang room service and ordered some hot milk. The Jury were to announce their verdict later that day. She couldn't bear to think what would happen if they found Don guilty. She felt utterly helpless. She switched on the TV. A picture of Madeline Whitney flashed up on the twenty four hour news. Kay hit the remote. She couldn't bear to hear any more. She switched to a late night movie, a B-movie, no brainer, with actors she'd never seen before. Perhaps it would stop her brain racing over the events of the trial. Despite the soporific film and the hot milk, sleep eluded her. She rose early, feeling shattered; showered, washed her hair and drank the disgusting instant coffee in her room, before heading, with a sense of foreboding, towards the High Court.

There were two factions outside the Court. Some were waving placards saying **ABORTION KILLS**, and **ABORTION CLAIMS TWO VICTIMS**. Others saying **ABORTION, A WOMAN'S RIGHT TO CHOOSE, CREIGHTON GUILTY**. A small group of people knelt, praying. Apparently they'd been there on an all-night, candlelight vigil. Scuffles began to break out, but the police reacted quickly, stepping in to separate the troublemakers.

Chapter forty-three

When Kay looked over at Don in the dock, she thought that he, too, hadn't slept. He looked pale and drawn. She wanted to put her arms round him. Instead, she bent forward, on the edge of her seat, as the Foreman of the Jury stood up.

The Judge looked over the top of his glasses.

'You have reached a verdict?'

'Yes, M'Lord,' the Foreman replied gravely.

'What is your verdict?'

'Guilty, M'Lord.'

Kay's heart sank to the pit of her stomach.

There was an immediate uproar in the court. The Judge banged his gavel and raised his voice above the tumult.

'The prisoner will rise.'

Don stood, his face impassive.

'Donald Joseph Creighton, you have been found guilty of the charge of attempted murder,' the Judge pronounced.

'Before I sentence you, I wish to say a few words. This has not been an easy case. Even allowing for the celebrity status of Miss Whitney, the difficult and unusual circumstances surrounding your birth have added to this trial being conducted in the media spotlight. I commend the jury for not permitting themselves to be swayed by the resultant circus. Donald Joseph Creighton, you took the law into your own hands. Psychiatric reports show that you are sane and fit to plead. You have condemned a gifted and talented woman to a life confined in a wheelchair. There is no justification in law for this type of action. I, therefore, sentence you to imprisonment for a period of ten years.'

Kay was unable to stop the tears coursing down her cheeks as Don was led away.

Chapter forty-four

The last four months had gone by as if in a dream, verging on a nightmare. Don still had the feeling that he was watching events happening to someone else. But when he woke up each morning, to the sounds of Johnnie Ferguson's snoring and stared at the ceiling of the tiny cramped cell they shared, he was brought back to reality with a depressing jolt. His cell-mate, who'd strangled his wife after a quarrel, was a man of few words. Time dragged by in a ritual of trying to eat the unpalatable food on offer, exercise yard, gym and his work in the library. The latter he quite enjoyed. He'd even requested paper and pen so that he might write, but the Muse seemed to be wary of prison life and had deserted him.

When he thought back to the night he'd been arrested, events were hazy. He remembered the dehumanising strip search; his first night in the medical wing on suicide watch. He hadn't felt suicidal, if they'd but known. Their precautions seemed unnecessary, in his detached state, but he guessed it must be standard procedure. He'd then been transferred to another prison, re-categorised because of the nature of his crime and had shared a cell with Ferguson ever since.

The latter got out of bed, scratched, farted and peed vigorously into the toilet bowl. He then squatted down on the seatless lavatory. Don was treated to a series of grunts. He turned his face to the wall. He'd never get used to this lack of privacy. Ferguson flushed the toilet and ambled over to the washbasin. The smell of his dump pervaded the air.

'Sorry 'bout that. Must have been the chilli.'

He turned back towards him, surprised to hear Ferguson speak.

His silence, hitherto, had suited Don. He, too, preferred the company of his own thoughts.

'Only another coupla months to put up wi' me,' the big man continued. The sense of impending freedom seemed to have loosened his tongue.

Chapter forty-five

Strapped into her wheelchair in the customised car, Madeline had never felt so alone. Since the terrible events in Edinburgh that had left her quadriplegic, she realised, in a way that she had never done before, how reliant on other people she was. Not merely for the day to day routine that had become her life back in New York, the staff who bathed, fed, turned her in the bed to prevent bed sores, wiped her bottom and the hundred and one things she had taken for granted. No, she was talking about friendship, real friendship. Sure, friends and colleagues from the studios had, initially, come around with flowers and sympathy, but those visits had become less and less frequent, before gradually tailing off altogether. No–one had volunteered to come with her today. True, she wasn't the easiest of patients. She'd always been a fiercely independent, private person. She railed against her helplessness in a way they found embarrassing. Staff had come and gone, at the end of their tether.

In driving her to the nursing home, Will was carrying out his last duty. Her two nurses had lifted Madeline from the bed with Will's help. He'd wheeled her from the house she loved, but would never see again. The property was already in the hands of her lawyer, ready to be sold. Having attended her for frequent chest and urinary infections, Doctor Schwartz, her physician, told her it was imperative she had continuity of medical care. He recommended Riverglade. The place was one of the few with doctors and nurses in attendance.

The Matron, Mrs Roche, came out to meet them. Riverglade was no stranger to celebrity. Many famous thespians had spent their last years there, but few as comparatively young and at the height of her career, as Madeline Whitney. Mrs Roche was not a cinema-goer but, even she knew of Madeline's fame. The case had been splashed all over the media and had caused a huge tidal wave of support for the actress. The public were fickle, however, and had moved on, after their initial sympathy.

'Welcome to Riverglade, Miss Whitney.' Madeline looked at the trim, capable-looking Matron. The woman's smile seemed genuine. Madeline made up her mind quickly about people. This one seemed ok. An attendant stepped forward to take over from Will, but the latter hung on to the handle of the wheelchair, as if reluctant to relinquish his duties.

'I'll take Miss Whitney inside, man.'

The Matron nodded briefly to the attendant, who stood aside as Will pushed Madeline's chair up the ramp into the building. He stopped inside the brightly lit hallway.

'May I come visit you Miss Whitney?' Madeline saw tears in the big man's eyes and nodded, unexpectedly fighting her own emotions. She knew Will had been consumed with guilt that he hadn't been able to save her that night. He had no need. She'd been the one who sent him away. He bent over her, took her hand in his big, capable ones.

'I'll see you, real soon.' With that, he turned on his heel and left. She felt suddenly and totally bereft.

Mrs Roche sensed her new patient's distress. She kept up a bright commentary as the attendant pushed Madeline around. The Nursing Home seemed smart and well-cared for.

Beautifully arranged flowers were everywhere. Their perfume mingled with the strong smell of air-freshener, no doubt concealing the odour of decrepitude, thought Madeline.

As they made their way along the corridor, they passed an old man with a stick, walking with the help of an orderly.

'Morning, James,' the Matron greeted him cheerily, but James, totally focussed on his journey, ignored them.

'Here we are Miss Whitney.' The Matron unlocked a door marked River View, giving Madeline the first sight of her new home. The room was ensuite, bright and cheerful, well furnished, exactly as shown in the brochure, but still with a slightly institutional feel.

'Would you wheel me to the window?' asked Madeline.

'Best view in the whole place,' Mrs Roche said, with a hint of pride.

The view had been the deciding factor. Madeline had been devastated at having to leave her beautiful, Long Island garden, her infinity pool. There was no way this view would recompense, but it was very attractive. A path led down through a beautifully manicured lawn, past a wild flowered meadow, to the river meandering below.

'Well, what do you think?'

Before Madeline could reply, there was a strange, high pitched sound behind her and an old woman, well dressed, wearing expensive jewellery, appeared, supported by a walking frame. She crossed purposefully to the window, started rapping on the glass, a slightly deranged look on her face.

'Mrs Goldberg, you're in the wrong room,' said Matron, with a hint of embarrassment.

The old lady looked round, confused, as an attendant apologetically appeared.

'Sorry about that. C'mon Esme.' Without a word, Mrs Goldberg obediently allowed herself to be led off. Madeline felt a chill in her heart.

Chapter forty-six

Don was lying awake on the top bunk. He'd been alone in his cell for two days following Ferguson's release. He'd relished the privacy but knew it was short lived. Space was at a premium; it seemed crime and punishment were the only growth industries in these troubled times. He'd been a little apprehensive. There were a lot of seriously disturbed guys in this place. He didn't relish being up close and personal with any of them. He'd been delighted when, earlier that day, the door to his cell had been unlocked and his old cell mate from his remand prison, Jimmy Dougan, had been ushered in.

Don was surprised to see him. Jimmy was a petty criminal.

Why had he been re-categorised?

'I decked that bastard, MacIntosh,' Jimmy explained. 'He was never off ma case.'

Don remembered the particular prison officer. He seemed to take a sadistic delight in goading Jimmy.

'Got an extra two year.' Jimmy added. 'Was worth it.'

Don knew this was bravado. The wee man hated being away from his wife and kids. He'd a good heart under the tough exterior. Don felt sharing a cell with him would make prison at least bearable. He lay awake, lost in his own thoughts, until the dawn broke.

'You sleepin?' Jimmy's voice floated up from the bunk below.

'No, can't, in this place.'

'Don't worry mate. You'll no' do ten years. Keep your nose clean, you'll be out in seven.'

'Don't care.'

'You will. After a coupla years in here, you'll be climbin' the walls. Take it from me.'

'So why d'you keep coming back?'

'Stupidity. Trying to get money for the wife and weans the easy way. Should know by now there's nae such thing.'

Chapter forty-seven

Back in New York, Madeline was in her own kind of prison, albeit of a more opulent nature. Riverdale functioned like a hotel cum hospital. Madeline had always enjoyed hotels. On her frequent world wide stops at the most luxurious palaces of sheer indulgence, she always refused staff offers to unpack on her behalf. Putting away her clothes seemed to Madeline akin to marking her territory. Now she had to watch helplessly as an attendant hung up and folded away.

In Riverglade, guests were free to roam about at will. This privilege, of course, was denied to her, as she was completely reliant on the staff for everything, from switching her radio on and off, to feeding her, wiping her mouth and every other region, even turning the pages of her book. She couldn't expect them to do the latter. Her luggage contained many talking books, but even they required someone to switch them off and on. When she got tired of hearing the recorded voice, she had to wait for someone to come in and stop the CD. The staff were very attentive but you couldn't expect them to be there twenty four seven, so you had to put up with the drone of the reader, long after your interest had tailed off. Same applied to radio or TV. You couldn't change channels. She found herself shouting in frustration at the TV, until a passing attendant appeared, apologetically.

The daily ritual of being hoisted on a series of pulleys from her bed to her wheelchair, then into her private bathroom, where she was showered sponged down, creamed, nappied and talced, like a helpless baby, had lost none of its humiliation. Perhaps, because the staff changed at regular intervals, she felt this sense of an overwhelming loss of any dignity; denuded before every new face. When an attendant wheeled her to the riverside on good days, she kept hoping she could, eventually, bribe one of them to leave her brake off so that she could roll forward into the merciful waters and oblivion.

Chapter forty-eight

Don and Jimmy had just returned from having breakfast. It was the one meal in the day that Don almost enjoyed. There wasn't much they could do wrong with cornflakes and a roll thinly spread with margarine. Coffee would have been nice but it wasn't on offer. The cell door was suddenly unlocked and a young officer, Dodds, came in.

'Creighton, you're on Reception as from today. You're a Passman. Look sharp.'

Don was surprised. No-one had mentioned him being taken off library duty. As far as he knew a Passman worked with the new entrants. It was a Trustee's job. A step-up he supposed. He made to follow the officer out when Jimmy hissed,

'Be careful!'

Don was puzzled. Jimmy touched his nose, meaningfully.

What was he warning him about? Don had no idea, but resolved to keep on his toes.

Twenty minutes later, Jimmy's warning became clear. Don was at Prison Reception, standing outside one of the tiny holding cells, known to the prisoners as dog boxes. He was holding a pile of street clothes, jeans, leather jacket, and boots. There was an urgent tap from inside the dog box. He looked through the glass at the, now naked, new inmate MacGurk, a lanky, undernourished looking guy with few teeth, despite his apparent youth. MacGurk held a small packet through the gap at the top.

'Take this through for us.'

'No way.' Don was adamant.

Another prisoner Passman, MacLeod, grabbed the packet and moved on, as MacGurk made his way to the prison showers.

The latter emerged a few minutes later; hair wet and grabbed his prison clothes from Don.

'Fuck you, Yank!' He almost spat the words.

Don was taken aback at the venom in his tone. MacLeod, winking at MacGurk, handed him his drugs back. MacLeod, unseen by Don, quickly slipped something into Don's pocket as he passed. MacLeod then ambled up to Prison Officer Dodds and muttered to him. They both cast a look over in Don's direction. Don, busy clearing up wet towels, didn't see their exchange. It was only when he felt a grip on his arm from Officer Dodds that he looked up.

'Against the wall Creighton,' Dodds ordered grimly.

He and another young officer searched efficiently through Don's pockets. It didn't take them long. Dodds removed a small packet of drugs from Don's pocket.

'You're in trouble, fella,' he said.

Chapter forty-nine

Madeline, surprisingly, had had a busy week. First a visit from the faithful Will. He sat there in the lounge, looking smaller out of his chauffeur's uniform. He'd got himself another job with a security firm and had come on his day off. Madeline appreciated his effort, as he was obviously uncomfortable seeing his former, dynamic, employer in this setting. He tried to talk to her, but it was a struggle. An attendant wheeled Maisie, a twisted looking, pathetic creature, to an adjoining seat. Maisie kept up a rhythmic drumming with her hands on the table in front of her. Madeline had got used to it, but it obviously upset Will. He made his excuses early and left.

Next day brought Annie Novak, Madeline's agent. She'd represented Madeline for over twenty years. Annie had a hard business streak, but her concern for Madeline was genuine. She'd flown over to Scotland twice to visit her in hospital. Some might have cynically said her concern was for her depreciating asset. Madeline had made a lot of money for Annie. The latter's plush LA offices on Wilshire Boulevard were testament to that, but Annie genuinely liked her client. They had lunch together whenever Madeline was available. They were alike in a lot of ways, hard to get to know, but with a direct, sometimes abrasive manner. Neither suffered fools gladly. Annie never tried to push Madeline into a movie purely for the fee. If she thought it was a poor quality screenplay she'd say so; advise her to pass on it. In Annie's estimation you were only as good as the material with which you had to work. She'd shaped Madeline's career very effectively. The quality of the work resulted in many awards, but only because her client embraced the challenge in each new role with total commitment. She had the uncanny ability to physically and vocally change in front of the camera, seemingly from the inside out. No easy feat. The camera could be merciless in spotting any false note, but truth was recognised to be at the heart of every Madeline

Whitney performance.

If Madeline was up for an Oscar her fellow actresses felt resignedly that they had little chance. No doubt in their uncharitable moments some of her competitors were a little pleased that she was now out of the running.

Annie had come to let Madeline know that she was still working on her behalf; in fact had an idea to put to her. When she'd finished the coffee the attendant had brought, as they sat out on the lawn in the spring sunshine, she raised the subject.

'TV wants to do a programme about you.'

Madeline raised her eyebrows.

'A kind of retrospective of your movies. The executive producer, Steven Rossiter, asked to come see you. Talk it over.'

'What do they want from me?'

'Background, input, I guess. He wouldn't be more specific.'

Madeline was wary. 'You think I should see him? In this place?'

Annie shrugged. 'Do no harm to talk. See what he has to say. They're talking high production values, a lot of money.'

Madeline had reluctantly agreed. She didn't really want reminders of her former glory. All that was irrevocably behind her. Hers wasn't a calm acceptance, more an inner rage, but there was nothing she could do about it. Christopher Reeve had spent his later life hoping for a cure. She wouldn't allow herself any optimism. That way led to disappointment.

She saw Steven Rossiter two days later. He had apparently been pressing Annie for an early meeting. He was ushered into Madeline's suite by the Matron herself. No doubt Matron liked television exposure, thought Madeline, cynically. You couldn't pay for that kind of advertising.

'Miss Whitney,' he advanced, hand outstretched. There was an awkward moment when he realised she couldn't raise her arm, and dropped his, feebly, at his side. He looked incredibly young to be making programmes, but television production was a young person's field. You were over the hill at fifty five. He was extremely courteous, had brought her flowers, carefully chosen ones, birds of paradise blooms, other exotics she could not name, but expensive, beautifully, creatively, wrapped; a still life almost. He was obviously out to impress.

'Has your agent told you anything about my proposal?'

It was a strange word, as if he was asking for her hand in marriage; a hand she could no longer extend.

'So it's just a proposal at this stage, my agent hasn't given you any indication as to whether I'd accept?'

'Absolutely not,' he assured, fearful of early rejection. He was all too aware of her formidable reputation where the media were concerned. She'd have to be courted carefully.

'Annie Novak wants to make sure; we both do,' he added hastily, 'that you're happy with the format of the programme.'

'So what exactly is the content of this programme going to be?'

'Well,' he began, with a hint of nervousness, 'it's going to be an in-depth look at the film career of Madeline Whitney, an analysis of your technique.'

'And who is going to be making this analysis?'

'Sheridan Hilton,' he named a prominent and respected film critic.

'Forgive me for saying so, Mr... eh Rossiter,' Madeline said, with a hint of weariness, 'but it sounds a little old hat! I can think of at least three previous programmes on the same subject. What is your particular angle?'

'We would want an input from you.'

'I had an input on two of the three I mentioned.'

There was a brief pause before Steven Rossiter answered,

'But those were made before…' He tailed off.

'Before I was crippled,' she answered sharply.

'Well, yes.'

'I get it, you want me to appear as I am today, in this vegetative state, while images of me as a young vibrant woman appear on the screen.'

'It would be handled extremely sensitively, Miss Whitney,' the young man assured 'your dignity is of paramount importance to us.'

'Don't you get it? I have no bloody dignity, now.'

'Miss Whitney'…he tried vainly to reason with her.

'That's it, isn't it?'

It all became clear to her.

Human interest. The public would watch, even those not particularly interested in film. They loved a victim. Like watching a car crash.

'Get out of here, now.'

'Please Miss Whitney,' he pleaded, wary of going back to his Commissioning Editor saying he'd blown it.

'Get out!' There was no mistaking the steely look in her eyes.

As the door closed behind him, she gave vent to the first tears of self-pity she'd shed.

Chapter fifty

Don was being escorted unceremoniously to the Prison Governor's office. Prison Officer Dodds tapped on the door and entered, ushering Don in front of him.

'Prisoner Creighton, sir,' he announced.

The Governor, a mild-mannered man, who looked like a Bank Manager, looked up gravely. 'Leave us, Mr Dodds, will you?'

As Dodds left, the Governor leant back in his chair for a moment, as if gathering his thoughts before telling Don his overdraft facility had been refused. He then leant forward, his elbows on the desk, hands together in almost a praying position, under his chin.

'I'm very disappointed in you, Creighton.'

He opened his hands, but left his finger tips together, as he surveyed the prisoner over the top of his spectacles.

'No previous convictions, not even a parking violation, yet you're now caught in possession. You must know that's a serious offence.'

Don looked away.

'Do you have a drug habit, Creighton?'

'No, sir.'

'We're not stupid in here. We know what goes on.' There was weariness in the Governor's tone, 'An incoming prisoner asks the Passman to bring something through before he's strip searched. It's a temptation which some give into. Is that what happened?'

Don hesitated before answering, 'I didn't bring them through.'

'So they were planted on you. Who by? Was it MacLeod?' the Governor persisted. 'Who did they come from?'

The merest flicker passed across Don's face.

The Governor felt a mounting frustration. How do you get through to these prisoners?

'Why are you being loyal to these men, Creighton? They fitted

148

you up. Thanks to them, you've lost your Trustee position on Reception. This could also cost you your parole. Ten years is a long time. Think about it.'

Don went back to his cell, lay on his bed looking at the four walls and, for the first time, allowed himself to think about Kay. Thoughts of her, what all this must have done to her, caused him pain. He usually tried to force all feelings for her from his mind. It had to be over between them. Anything else was sheer selfishness on his part. He couldn't expect her to wait ten years.

Chapter fifty-one

Kay gripped the wheel of her car and let out a long slow expiration of breath, to steady herself. It had been a difficult few hours. On an assignment for her newspaper, she had spent the morning on a military base interviewing a number of soldiers' wives whose husbands had returned from combat in Iraq and Afghanistan with not only physical, but mental injuries.

The last woman, Mrs Alvirez had agreed with the other wives that the latter was the most difficult to deal with.

'Juan can cope with losing his leg,' she said, 'but not his buddies. He keeps blaming himself. There was nothin' he could do. He didn't plant the bomb, but he doesn't see it that way.'

The woman had broken down sobbing. She told Kay of the strain post-traumatic stress was putting on their marriage.

'He's a totally different person now. One that I don't recognise. It's his brain that's really injured, that's the hard part. The part you don't see. All you see is the effect it's having on him, on your marriage, on the kids.'

Back at her office Kay looked over the notes she'd taken that morning. There was a pattern to the symptoms that their husbands had displayed.

'Avoidance' was a word she'd heard frequently and underlined in her notebook.

'He won't drive the car, no more,' Mrs Bruckerman had said. 'At first he would, but he kept looking up at the buildings, all nervous like, looking for snipers. On the way to the grocery store for Heaven's sake.'

Kay thought of Don, of his gradual reluctance to get back behind the wheel of a car after the accident that killed his parents. She looked at the 'other common symptoms' they'd mentioned. 'Feeling detached' was number two on her list.

'He never hugs me or the kids any more,' Mrs Alvirez had said tearfully. 'Can't remember when we last made love. It's as if Juan doesn't have any feelings for us now. It's like someone has pressed a switch and shut down his emotions.'

Their words really hit home with Kay. They could be talking about Don here. She had been finding life very difficult since the trial. No-one seemed to understand. The media hadn't helped. They had painted Don as a psychopath, bent on vengeance, who'd stalked Madeline both in the States and in Scotland. In their mind, the whole thing had been premeditated. He had been the one sending the threatening letters to her. He'd followed her to Scotland, knowing her security might not be as rigorous and had seized the opportunity to exact his revenge. Of course, those who knew him, could not believe him capable of such an action, but there were one or two at work who believed all they read, ironic as it seemed, working for a newspaper. The whisperings had got to her. She'd taken leave, gone back to her family in Boston. Her folks loved Don, but their faith was a little shaken. Why did he keep refusing to see Kay when she went over to Scotland? She had explained her theory of post–traumatic stress. They were sympathetic, but not totally convinced.

'He's your fiancé, for Heaven's sake,' her mother said. 'He must know you're on his side. Why won't he talk to you?'

'Surely, the courts would know if he was suffering from psychological problems?' her straight talking, ex-army Dad said. 'I mean, these guys have got shrinks on tap.'

Her sisters were sympathetic, but non-committal. She couldn't bear the fact that even her family were allowing themselves to be influenced by the media. Using the excuse of pressure of work, she had cut short her Boston trip and flown back to New York.

She lifted her notebook, crossed the room and tapped the door of the Editor's office. Fortunately the one person whose faith in Don was unshakeable was Harry Silverman. Harry prided himself on his ability to read people. He'd known Don since he came to the paper, fresh from University, on work experience. He liked the young man immediately; a bright, keen, Grade A student. Harry had no second thoughts about offering Don a permanent position at the end of his internship. As Kay talked over her morning interviews with the soldiers' wives, he was keenly aware of her struggle to fight back tears.

'There are so many parallels with Don here,' she said.

'Is he still not answering your letters?' he asked gently.

She shook her head. She felt numb. She'd gone over this in her mind so many times.

'Would it help if I wrote to him again?'

'I honestly don't know, Harry.'

'I'll tell him the truth. You've used up all your holidays and you're taking some unpaid leave to go back again to Scotland to try and visit him.'

She raised her eyebrows.

'You think I should try again?' What if he doesn't... ?' She tailed off.

'He's got to. I'll point out it's his goddam duty to meet you. He owes you that.'

She spent that night arranging flights and accommodation near to the prison. She'd turn up there every visiting day. She had to talk to Don, make him see sense.

Her frustration was turning to a kind of anger, fuelling a steely determination. Their future was worth fighting for.

Chapter fifty-two

Don had been moved to the gardening unit, temporarily, he was told, before being assigned new duties. He hadn't yet come to grips with the system. They knew he could be trusted as a Passman. MacLeod's cell had been searched and they'd found drugs behind the cistern. They knew he'd planted hash on Don, so why the move to Gardening? To be honest, he was grateful for the move. His cellmate, Jimmy, warned that a number of the prisoners now had it in for him. He was seen as a grass, the worst offence you can commit in prison. He didn't want any more incidents of that nature and as a Passman, you were in a no-win situation, condemned by the inmates if you didn't help them smuggle in drugs and punished by the prison authorities if you did. As a cub reporter he'd written a huge exposé of the drugs scene in New York. He hated what drug dependency did to people. He was aware that half of the inmates wouldn't be behind bars if it wasn't for the crimes they committed to feed their habit. However, the move to Gardening, albeit temporary, was a welcome one. He'd never done anything but cut the lawn back home. When Don was a boy, his parents had a gardener, Carlos, who'd been with them for years. He had a real bond with nature, could coax anything to grow, but the old Mexican gradually slowed down. As his arthritis took hold, he was content to potter about, weeding and burning rubbish, so the lawn became Don's pocket money earner. That way it saved Carlos's pride. Now the chance to be out in the fresh air amongst plants and flowers gave almost a semblance of freedom.

It was a beautiful late spring day. There was even a bit of warmth in the sunshine. When he looked around him at the tulip beds, he could forget where he was, for a moment, almost ignore the watchful eye of the guard. He was gently treading the soil around a row of young birch trees he'd planted, when Stewart, one of the older officers, exchanged a few words with the guard before coming up to him.

'That fiancée of yours has got some staying power.'

Don looked up, questioningly.

'She's back again,' Stewart continued. 'Have I to tell her you still don't want to see her?'

Don's hesitation was only momentary.

'Yeah.' He continued to tread the soil round the sapling.

'Just think,' said Stewart, after a moment, that'll be a big tree by the time you get out of here.'

He walked away, whistling quietly, but his words struck home. Don's face changed. He hurried after the officer.

It was an open visit. Other prisoners, with their families, were there, grouped around the room. Jimmy sat with his wife and little girls, talking animatedly. He looked up, surprised, as Don came through, and then followed his glance to Kay, looking tense, but trying to smile, as she rose to greet him. She tried to hug him but the guard looked over warningly. It was a favourite device for passing drugs, though these were considered to be the prisoners without a habit. The addicted ones were on closed visits, talking to their families through a screen. Perhaps this guy considered him to be still under suspicion. For whatever reason, Don froze. Kay, disappointed, but sensing Don's discomfort, reluctantly let him go. They both sat down.

'It's so good to see you, Don.'

He found it hard to meet her eye. She touched his chin, his early beard.

'This is new.'

'Yeah... something to do.'

She looked at him searchingly, trying to drink in every detail of the face she loved so much.

'How are you?'

Don shrugged. 'You know.'

'No I don't, Don. I've no idea. You refuse to see me, don't

answer my letters.'

She found it difficult to keep anger from creeping into her voice.

'I've been going out my mind worrying.'

'I'm sorry.' He looked away as he said the words.

She couldn't believe that was all he had to say. Didn't he realise what he'd put her through? He was normally such an empathetic person. What the hell was happening to him?

Whatever it was, he was obviously still in some kind of trauma. She realised she had to tread carefully. She didn't want to lose him.

'Doesn't matter. You're here, now.' She made her tone deliberately bright. 'I'd some vacation time left, managed to get a cheap flight. Thought I'd have one final try.'

She took his hand. 'I love you, sweetheart.'

He moved his hand away. 'That's what it has to be.'

'What?'

'Final.'

'What are you saying?'

'I'm in here for ten years. Go away, Kay.' His face was strained, serious. 'Don't waste your life.'

'You think I'm just going to give up on you. What do you take me for?'

She no longer even attempted to hide her anger.

'Yeah… well. My feelings have changed.' He looked away again as he said the words.

'I don't believe you.'

'You better.' He stood up, dismissively, made to go.

'Just a minute!' Her raised, irate tone stopped him in his tracks. 'What do you think my feelings have gone through? The man I thought was gentle and kind tries to kill someone?'

'So you convicted me too,' he said bitterly.

'When I try to see you to find out what really happened you block me out.' She saw the sudden look of pain cross his face. When she continued, her tone was gentler.

'Why didn't you tell me about Miami? Such a terrible thing to find out. You should have talked to me about it.'

'What difference does it make? I survived.'

'So why bury yourself now?'

He turned away.

She had to get through to him. There was desperation in her voice.

'Don! You must appeal against your sentence.'

He turned back to her, shook his head.

'No!'

'Don't you care what happens to you?'

'Not anymore.'

'Why?'

'You said it yourself. I tried to kill someone.'

'So now you're killing our future?' her eyes flashed angrily. 'The children we might have had!'

Don looked at her sadly for a moment before turning to the officer, indicating that, for him, the visit was over.

Chapter fifty-three

He was grateful for the exercise period, walking round the yard with Jimmy in companionable silence, each lost in his own thoughts. Jimmy was subdued after family visits. The sight of his young kids seemed to reinforce what he was missing. The little girls clung to him as they said their goodbyes. The eldest one, Debbie, talked non-stop during the visit, filling him in about school. He always boasted to Don that she had brains.

'Takes after the wife, thank God.'

Debbie had cried when it was time to leave. The middle one, Katie, almost refused to look at him, throughout the visit. Only when she was leaving, did she give vent to her emotion. Strange, because she spent the hour apparently engrossed in dressing and re-dressing her Barbie doll. The younger girl, a beautiful little kid with blonde curls, seemed too young to understand why her father didn't leave with them.

Don's thoughts, of course, were of Kay. He felt absolute despair at his situation. He'd really messed up both of their lives. Jimmy seemed to read his mind. He suddenly broke the silence.

'That fiancée of yours is a lovely lookin' lassie.'

Don nodded.

'Think she'll wait for you?'

'Hope not.'

'You don't mean that, man. She's a pure doll.'

'So why should she waste her life waiting on me?'

'Cause she loves ye, ya daft bugger.'

Before Don could reply, the breath was suddenly taken from his body as Armstrong's massive bulk barged into him.

Don turned on him angrily, but Jimmy pulled him away.

Armstrong glared over at Don, but did nothing, aware of the watchful eyes of the supervising prison officers.

'Word is you grassed up his mates,' said Jimmy, sotto voce, 'I've heard him mouthing off in the kitchen, so watch your back.'

Chapter fifty-four

Don didn't have long to wait before Armstrong made his move. For some reason, known only to the powers that be, Don was transferred to kitchen duties to work alongside Jimmy. Unfortunately, Armstrong was also a kitchen worker. Don tried to give him a wide berth. Apart from the latter's threatening presence, Don enjoyed kitchen duties, particularly the good-natured banter from the other prisoners as they lined up for meals.

'Whit? Nae Kentucky fried chicken?'

'Black-eyed peas?'

'C'mon Yank, you can dae better than this.'

Don, smiling, put out a portion of chips.

'Hey? Nae mair chips?' this from a young, fresh faced kid who seemed to live on nothing else but French-fries.

'They're just coming,' Don smiled.

'Aye, so's Christmas. C'mon man! I'm pure starving!'

Don, unable to resist the pleading in the kid's voice, crossed into the kitchen where Jimmy was re-filling food containers.

'Those French fries ready, Jimmy?'

'Armstrong, how's it comin?' Jimmy called over.

The big man looked up from frying a vat of chips.

'Come and get them,' he replied, a smile playing about his lips. As Don approached the chip container, Armstrong dipped the scoop into the bubbling mixture, deliberately splashing a ladleful of boiling hot fat over Don's bare arm. Don yelled in pain.

'Ya bastard! I saw that,' said Jimmy, running over to Don. Prison Officer Dodds rushed over.

'Right, Infirmary! Armstrong, you're in deep trouble!'

'It was an accident, Mr Dodds,' Armstrong was all innocence. As Dodds helped Don out, Armstrong put his fingers to his mouth, warningly and made a gesture to Jimmy, as if to slash his face if he talked.

Chapter fifty-five

Apart from the pain in his arm from the red, angry burn, Don really appreciated his brief sojourn in the Infirmary; any change was a welcome one from the monotony of prison routine. He even managed to get through a novel from the prison library, *Our Man in Havana*, as the staff were more relaxed over Lights Out.

He and Kay had visited Havana the year before. He had always meant to read the novel. He liked Graham Greene's style. He had tried to buy it from several book stores and second hand bookstalls in Havana, but with no success. Don loved reading novels set in the country he was visiting. They evoked the atmosphere of the place and fed the imagination in a way that dry travel books failed to do. They'd had a wonderful time there, hiring a car and driver to take them around other parts of Cuba. They spent a lovely romantic night in the charming town of Trinidad, which, after the tourists had left, returned to its own particular, colonial-style charm. They'd danced the night away at one of the many salsa clubs, their efforts on the dance floor put to shame by an elderly lothario in a white suit and dyed black hair, who spun all the young girls round the dance floor in a spectacular display of natural rhythm, grace and sensuality.

He must have fallen asleep, dreaming of Kay and beautiful white Cuban beaches, but woke up with Jimmy bending over him, bearing a tray with lunch on it.

'Grub's up. How's the arm?'

'I'll survive.' He raised himself to a sitting position, careful not to lean on his throbbing arm.

'Aye, you just might. Armstrong is being transferred to Peterhead.'

He never ceased to marvel at how well informed Jimmy was on prisoners' movements, but his information always proved to be reliable. A shadow crossed Don's face.

'His sidekicks are still here.'

'They'll no' do nothing,' said Jimmy, 'Armstrong's the muscle.'

Don was, unexpectedly, discharged from the Infirmary later that evening. A prisoner had cut his own wrists and required the bed. As Don entered his cell, Jimmy turned away, but not quickly enough to hide the fact that he'd been crying. He always seemed such an upbeat little character that Don was totally taken aback. He wasn't quite sure how to deal with it.

'You ok?' he asked, awkwardly.

Jimmy wiped his eyes quickly. 'The wife's pregnant.'

'Right.'

'She's had a scan. It's a wee boy...'

'Congratulations.' Don shook his hand.

'Always wanted a wee boy... after the three lassies, you know.'

Don handed him a cigarette. 'Celebration time then,' he said, smiling.

When Jimmy answered, his voice was almost breaking.

'I'm gonny be in this fuckin' place. No seein' him growin' up nor nothin.'

Don almost put his hand on the little guy's shoulder, but drew back. His own emotions were in such a mess that he no longer knew how to deal with other people's. He crossed to his bed, picked up a letter lying there, with an American postmark and a familiar hand. Don stared at it long and hard. Jimmy turned to look at him.

'You should write back to Kay.'

'Butt out, Jimmy.'

'She's serving a sentence as well.'

The remark hit home. Don slowly opened the letter.

Chapter fifty-six

Madeline sat in her wheelchair in the sunshine of the conservatory, looking out listlessly. She had intended asking to be wheeled into the garden, but the inmates who ventured out, came back in quickly, saying there was a deceptively cold breeze. It was only April, after all. An elderly woman, Bessie, a relative newcomer, with Alzheimer's, lay sleeping in an armchair. Oh for some real human contact, she thought. Was this it? Life crawling by. An inner rage ate away at her. Why me? she asked God at regular intervals, but never got an answer.

The conservatory doors opened and a stocky, youngish man, Alan Goodwright, dressed in a sharp, dark blue business suit, came over to her. She suddenly remembered Matron telling her a Mr Goodwright had telephoned to say he was coming. Madeline had forgotten when. One day in this place drifted into another.

'Hi, Miss Whitney.' He smiled, showing perfect, expensive dentistry.

'Morning Alan. It is morning isn't it?'

'Eh… no. It's two o'clock,' he said, a little awkwardly.

Was her mind going now? Alan wondered. He hoped not. He needed her to fully comprehend what he was about to tell her.

'I lead such an exciting life in here, I lose all track of time,' said Madeline wryly.

He pulled a chair over to her, sat down, opened his briefcase and extracted some papers. The sleeping woman suddenly let out a gentle snore. Alan looked up.

'Sorry, Miss Whitney, maybe you wanted to discuss this in your room?'

'Bessie has no interest in my financial affairs,' Madeline gave a rueful smile, 'Nor in anything else for that matter.'

'See you haven't lost your sense of humour.'

'Believe me; you need one in this place.'

Good, he thought. A perfect opening.

'You could move somewhere else.'

'You're not going to go on about that again. I've told you, this nursing home is the best... of its kind.'

'And the most expensive.'

'So! What else can I do with my money?'

He took a deep breath. It was time for truth. No sense in treading carefully round the subject.

'Miss Whitney, the five years you've spent in this place have eaten quite a hole in your capital.'

Had it really been only five years since she came here? Madeline thought. It felt like twenty. 'You're not telling me I'm broke, are you? I've earned a fortune.'

'But your ex took a lot of your capital in alimony.'

'Don't remind me.' Her tone was bitter.

Her ex, Jeremy Wright, was an asshole. There was no other word for him. He'd been a struggling actor when she met him. Very soon after their marriage, he'd happily given up the struggle and been content to live on her success. Friends had warned her about him, but she loved him, so ignored their criticisms. She had absolute faith in him, until she knew better. True, he'd tried a couple of ventures, writing, directing, but had shown little talent for either. The one thing he had, the quality that attracted her in the first place, was total self belief. Like a lot of talented actors, Madeline was always full of insecurity and doubt about her own abilities. Never being satisfied. Always wanting another take. Jeremy was the exact opposite. Unfortunately, his belief in his own talent was totally misplaced. He, or rather she, had financed a couple of films which he'd written. They sank without trace. One even won a Rotten Tomatoes award at Cannes. God knows what he was doing now. She'd heard nothing. Not so much as a sympathy card from him since her attack. Probably living it up somewhere with a nubile teenager on her money. He had developed a penchant for young girls. No doubt they'd allow him to control, something Madeline fiercely resisted, hence the divorce.

'Look, let me lay it on the line here, Miss Whitney. You're still a comparatively young woman. You could live another thirty years, more maybe.'

'If I thought that I'd top myself,' she answered feelingly.

Alan looked at her, slightly taken aback, before he continued.

'If you multiply what you've already spent in here, by six, your finances will be severely strained. And charges keep going up.'

'What are you suggesting?'

'Take out a civil action against Don Creighton .'

'I've told you before,' she said, vehemently, 'I want nothing from him.'

'Then your only alternative is to find more modest residential care.' He removed several brochures from his bag.

'This is information on less expensive places. As your Financial Advisor, I'd be failing in my duty if I didn't urge you to think about it.'

'Looks as if I have no choice,' said Madeline, with a sinking heart.

Chapter fifty-seven

Kay had put off the moment of returning home to Boston, but could delay it no longer. Her older sister, Clare, wanted her to be godmother to the new baby, their third child, Dominic. She and Clare had always been close. The latter was the first to call her, on that terrible day, when Don was arrested; commiserating with her, totally baffled by the turn of events, saying the family all felt it had been a ghastly mistake, that Don would be out soon, when the true culprit was apprehended. Now, five and a half years later, Clare never mentioned him. Like the rest of the family, she just didn't know what to say, knowing that Kay was steadfastly standing by him.

Kay was aware, however, of the hesitation in her sister's voice when she mentioned that the godfather would be Greg Dempsey. Before she could react, Clare added, in a breathless rush, that she knew this might be a little awkward, but Greg was one of her husband's oldest friends and he wanted to have him. Her voice had tailed off. Kay reassured her that whatever she and Greg had been to one another, it was all in the past. Clare sounded relieved; assuring Kay that she was pretty certain Greg felt the same. He'd been dating a really pretty nurse called Judy for almost six months. She and Bill had invited them over for dinner several times. They seemed happy together and according to her husband, it was pretty serious. Kay was surprised at how this news affected her. Her feelings were very mixed, pleased that Greg had found someone, but sorry for herself. She felt suddenly bereft and couldn't understand why.

She'd known Greg since High School. They'd started dating in their last year. They'd gone their separate ways when she left for University, but had kept in contact, telephoned regularly. He wasn't much of a letter writer. When she'd taken up a position back home in a Boston newspaper, they had resumed their relationship. He'd been working in a garage when Kay left for University. Now he owned his own. He was a smart guy, but not in an academic way. He was funny, loving, and decent; everything you'd want in a husband, but it wasn't enough for Kay. Quite apart from the fact that she was ambitious, not ready to settle down before she'd made any kind of mark in the world, they weren't on the same level, mentally. She hated herself for thinking like that. It sounded like intellectual snobbery. Greg would probably have attained University if he'd applied himself. It just wasn't what he wanted. She found there were areas she didn't discuss with him, art, literature, politics even. He just wasn't interested. She felt that, if she married him, the intellectual gap would widen, perhaps create a permanent rift. She didn't articulate these fears when she broke up with him. It would have sounded so patronising. She didn't really give him a reason, which left him even more devastated. As the weeks went by, she missed him dreadfully. She still loved him, but told herself she was doing the right thing, letting her head rule her heart.

There had been plenty of relationships after Greg, but it wasn't until she met Don that she knew why she'd waited. He was everything that Greg was, but so much more. At the thought of him now, her heart gave a wrench and despair returned.

Her mother had decided to hold a barbecue the night before the christening. Trying vainly to make small-talk, Kay felt like running back to her room and hiding. She sensed the awkwardness amongst her relatives as they spoke to her. There had never been any scandals of this magnitude in the Prentice family. She still wore her engagement ring, a fact not missed by any of her female relatives. There had been a much publicised television documentary the week before on the subject of stalkers. Pundits had been wheeled into the studio to discuss the rise in the phenomenon. Inevitably it had included footage about Don and Madeline Whitney, showing Don being led into the Edinburgh High Court in handcuffs and the sensationalist headlines on the Scottish billboards at the time.

Stalker preyed on Hollywood star
American stalker jailed for Madeline attack

They'd quoted court extracts from the trial showing Don had admitted he'd seen all her films and her Broadway performances, clear evidence, they stated of 'unhealthy obsession,' omitting, of course, that it was an integral part of his job as an Arts Correspondent.

Obviously many of the relatives and friends at the barbecue had seen the documentary. Kay was aware of the mutterings, although they studiously avoided any mention of Don when talking to her. She felt like a grieving widow, where no one referred to the deceased, denying they'd ever existed for fear of upsetting her. She took over from her father at the barbecue. There she could, at least, keep her conversation restricted.

'Steak, hamburger, sausages? Got some nice salmon steaks here.'

She had just filled half a dozen plates and was barbecueing more food, in anticipation, when she became aware of a familiar figure standing there.

'How are you, Kay?'

He was looking older, distinguished even. It suited him. She muttered some conventionally appropriate reply. Greg gazed at her steadily.

'How are you, really?' he said quietly.

'Hellish.'

'Can't be easy for you.'

'It's your worst nightmare.'

He reached for her hand.

'If there's anything I can do for you, anything. You know you only have to ask.'

Judy, his girl-friend, suddenly appeared. He introduced them both. Kay was sure the girl must know the history between herself and Greg. She hadn't imagined the slightly wary look in Judy's eyes, thinly disguised in the conventions of social intercourse. Kay avoided him for the rest of the evening. She had no wish to tread on anyone's toes.

Chapter fifty-eight

Next day, of course, Greg was impossible to avoid. As godfather and godmother they had been cast in leading roles. As she entered St Peter's Church with the baptismal party, for the eleven o'clock Mass, Kay felt a little uncomfortable. She had been raised as a Catholic, but a long time had elapsed since she'd put a foot in a Catholic Church. Not that she had rejected the Church's dogma, as such, but she had suddenly become aware that her grip on faith was a very tenuous one. Her attendance at Sunday Mass, she felt, was merely a kind of fire insurance, no doubt a throwback to her Junior School education where the school chaplain was a Redemptorist, very hot on hell and damnation.

When her family all filed out to receive Communion, she was the only one left in the pew. She felt all eyes were upon her. As the moment for the baptism approached, she was grateful for Greg's comfortingly assured presence at her side. Together, they approached the font. As the priest motioned her to unwrap little Dominic's shawl, she felt a sudden rush of responsibility for the little creature, who cried out in surprise at the sudden splash of cold water rudely awakening him from his sleep. Kay quickly wrapped him up again, held her to him, comfortingly. The baby snuggled into her. She looked up and caught an unmistakable tenderness in Greg's eyes. She wasn't sure if the feelings were directed at her or the little boy.

They stood together afterwards, with Clare, Bill and the new baby, resplendent in his christening clothes, as cameras flashed. Kay found Greg's proximity slightly disconcerting. She moved away to join a group of cousins as soon as the photography was over. She was aware of Judy crossing over to Greg, hanging on to his arm and his every word. For some inexplicable reason Kay found her proprietorial manner irritating. She was immediately annoyed at herself. What the hell did she expect? Greg to be hanging on a hook in case she deigned to change her mind? She realised that the only reason these thoughts impinged on her consciousness, was that she was lonely. Nearly six years without Don were taking their toll. She'd never stopped loving him, but it didn't fill the empty hole in her life. For a brief moment, she envied Judy.

Chapter fifty-nine

Don was in the library, giving Jimmy a little space. It was the day of the latter's release. He was packing up his few possessions. He'd talked about nothing else for the past six months, marking off the days on the calendar hanging on their cell wall. Don was pleased for him, but saddened. He felt he wouldn't have got through the last five and a half years if it wasn't for the little guy's company. They were from totally disparate backgrounds, not just geographical, but there was empathy and a bond between them. He glanced at his watch. Nearly time.

When Don got back to his cell, Jimmy was taking down the last of his photographs. Officer Johnson opened the door, stuck his head in.

'Ready?'

'Give us five minutes, Mr Johnson?'

Jimmy smiled at the photograph of his son, blowing out candles on his birthday cake. The little boy was dressed in a builder's yellow jacket which reached to his ankles and a hard hat. He apparently was crazy about the TV programme, 'Bob the Builder'. The outfit was a cheap birthday present, according to his wife, obtained by her brother who worked on a building site.

'The wife says the wee fella's talked about nothin' else but showing me his building gear.'

'Not every day your Dad comes home,' said Don, smiling.

'My poor lassies have seen me comin' and goin' all their lives.'

There was a catch in Jimmy's voice.

'Not any more, huh?'

'Swear on my mother's grave. I'll no be back.'

He put the photograph in his bag and turned to Don.

'Well, big man.'

Don held out his hand. Jimmy ignored it and gave him a hug.

171

'Gonna miss you' said Don. 'Even if I didn't know what the hell you were saying half the time.'

Jimmy was surprised at this admission. Perhaps he'd got through to the big Yank, after all. God knows, it wasn't for lack of trying. He was convinced Don should never have been in prison. The guy was honest and decent. He would never knowingly harm anyone. Jimmy could say that about few of his fellow inmates, despite their protestations of innocence and bleatings about miscarriages of justice. The little man was no psychiatrist, but to him, Don was boxed in emotionally. If ever there was a case for counselling, Don was it. Time to give it one final try.

'Listen, Don… get mad at me if you want, but I'm gonny say this. You need to get yourself sorted, man.'

Don turned away. Jimmy sighed in frustration.

'There's what I mean. Soon as the conversation gets anyway personal, the fuckin' shutters come doon. I know what you're goin' through.'

'How could you possibly…?'

'Cause I've been there,' Jimmy interrupted, 'wi' the guilt trip. It's taken me a long time to get over it. It's only now I can tell maself it wisnae ma fault.'

Don looked at him quizzically. Jimmy had never mentioned anything of this in the five and a half years they'd shared a cell.

'You're no the only one that bottles things up.' It was as if Jimmy had just read his thoughts.

The wee man sat down on the edge of his bed.

'I've been breakin' into folks' hooses since I was about seventeen. Before that it was a bit of shopliftin'. We never had nothin' in oor hoose,' he said defensively. 'The auld man was a drunk. Any money he had, he drank it - a right waster! Somebody had to go oot and get money. I was the eldest, so it was up to me.

Had he never thought of work? Don thought to himself.

Again it was as if the wee guy had read his thoughts.

'Work was a four letter word roon ma way,' Jimmy grinned ruefully. 'My Da didnae work, neither did his brothers. I'd nae role models, according to ma social worker. Anyway I'm no' makin' excuses... I was a bad lot. Didnae think I was, mind you. The way I looked at it, I only stole from rich folk, broke into the fancy big hooses. Anything I took they'd have it insured. They insurance fuckers are robbers tae, so they could afford it from the profits they made, so I never felt I was doin' anythin' wrong... until ma second last job.'

He took a cigarette out of his pocket, halved it and gave the other half to Don. Don lit both and listened curiously.

'It was a big house, Morningside, posh bit of Edinburgh. I'd sussed it oot. An auld couple lived there. I'd be in and oot while they were asleep, that was the plan.' He drew on his cigarette.

'I broke in downstairs, nae bother, jemmied the kitchen door, nae alarms, nothin.' Went through every drawer, livin' room, sitting room, lookin' for cash, never found a thing. Aw the ornaments they had was junk so I had to go upstairs. I'm creepin' up this big staircase, gets to the top and this young guy's staunin' there, purple wi' anger... I wisnae to know... their son was stayin' with them for a coupla days. Well, he makes a grab for me. I try to pull mysel' free and the two of us fall down the stairs. I jump up but he grabs ma leg and the two of us start wrestling about. Then this quavery old voice says, 'Stop that! The police are on their way.' He wiped his mouth, nervously. Don could see Jimmy was reliving the moment as he continued. 'The old dear, his Ma, is at the top of the stairs, so I gie him a shove and leg it out the door. I'm haulfway doon the street when the police car comes roaring towards me and I'm arrested. Next thing I'm up in court charged wi' manslaughter.'

'You killed the guy?' Don asked incredulously.

'Naw, his mother dropped dead wi' the upset of it all, about five minutes after I left. The Prosecution said I'd brought on her heart attack.' He looked up at Don, shaking his head. 'I'm tellin' you man, they tried to throw the book at me. Apparently she had been her husband's carer. He had Parkinson's Disease. The Prosecutor was laying it on thick. The auld man had to go into a home now that he'd lost his carer. The son lived abroad, couldnae look after him.' He drew on his cigarette again. 'My mindless act had destroyed the lives of two innocent people,' according to their bastard of a lawyer.' He stubbed out his cigarette.

'If you'd seen the hate in the eyes of the jury, man. I was lucky the mother had a history of heart disease otherwise I'd have been an old man before I got out the jail.'

He looked up at Don who was taking a final draw before extinguishing his cigarette.

'But you know, I told myself I deserved to be stuck inside for the rest of my life. If I hadnae broke into their place, they two old folk would still be in their hoose thegither. I'd never really thought about my victims before. Now I couldnae think about anything else.' He stood up.

'I'm tellin' you man. It really got to me. I couldnae eat. I couldnae sleep. I thought I was going off ma heid! When the wife and kids came to see me I hardly said two words to them.'

Don looked at him, surprised.

'This was before I knew you. On my previous stretch. Honest injun Don, I was a bit of a nutter. Aw closed in on maself. Wouldnae open up to anybody. Eventually the wife got fed up wi' it. She stopped bringing the kids. That shook me. She said ' What's the point? You don't speak to them. I'm no' bringin' them up here again until you see somebody. A shrink or something.'

'And did you?' Don asked.

'Naw, I just thought it oot masel. Well that's no quite true. I did talk it over with the padre. Just talking it over wi' somebody helped. It really did, man.'

He crossed to where Don stood at the window.

'I know this whole carry on wi' your mother did your heid in too, but it's past.'

The big man turned away from him, but Jimmy was relentless. He'd seen a chink in Don's emotional armour.

'Cancel and carry on, as my social worker used to say. Only useful piece of advice the wee shite ever gied me.'

'I'll try,' said Don hoarsely.

Jimmy gripped his arm, forcing Don to turn and face him.

'Don't try. Do it! You've got to learn to forgive her!'

'It's me I can't forgive,' said Don brokenly.

Officer Johnson reappeared. Jimmy went to the cell door, turned back.

'Think about it,' he said.

Don stood at the window for a long time, his emotions in turmoil. In six years he hadn't allowed himself to think about Madeline. It was too painful to revisit.

From his viewpoint, he could just see the corner of the garden, where he planted the sapling, now a tree.

Chapter sixty

Kay was sitting at her office computer, researching an article on Obama's F.O.C.A. legislation, when the phone rang.

'Kay?'

She recognised the voice immediately, but hid her surprise.

'Greg, how are you?'

'Fine. Hope you don't mind me calling, but I'm in New York, seeing one of my suppliers. Wondered if you'd like to have dinner with me tonight?'

She hesitated for a moment.

'Please say, yes. I hate eating alone. Like poor Johnny no-pals.'

'Can't have that,' she smiled. 'Where do you want to eat?'

'Somewhere in the Village? You'll know the restaurants better than me.'

She suggested La Belle France, an unpretentious little place with excellent food and friendly staff. They agreed to meet there at eight. She was going to suggest he called at her apartment for a drink first, but thought better of it. She put the phone down, a little disconcerted.

'You're looking a bit flushed,' said Janet, from across the desk. 'Everything ok?'

'Yeah,' said Kay. 'That was Greg.'

'Your ex?' Janet was agog.

Kay had told her about the christening three months earlier and the little frisson between her and Greg. Janet MacGarrity was a woman you could trust. It went no further. She'd been a rock to Kay over the past six years since Don's imprisonment. One of the few people in whom she confided.

'He's in town on business. Just wanted to meet up.'

'Yeah, right,' said Janet, cynically. 'You believe that?'

'Sure. His business has expanded now. He has dealerships, is into financing. He's done pretty well for himself.'

'Get in there,' said Janet.

'I'm not interested.'

'Really? Well tell him you've got a pal.'

Despite Kay's professed lack of interest she dressed with care, in a little black number which showed off her shoulders, her best feature. She walked the few blocks to the restaurant, feeling slightly apprehensive. He was already there, seated at a table, drinking a beer, wearing a well cut business suit in light grey. She was glad she'd made a little effort. He rose to meet her with a broad grin. She offered her cheek to him, but he looked at her appraisingly, pulled her into a bear like hug.

'You look fantastic.'

It wasn't until she'd downed her first glass of wine that she relaxed a little. Greg was good company. Always had been.

'How's Judy?' She felt she had to ask.

'Great,' he smiled. 'She's been promoted. She's a terrific girl. The patients love her. Everybody does.'

Including you? she wondered. If so why are you having dinner with me? For old times sake? She put these niggling questions out of her mind and gave herself up to enjoying the evening. She'd forgotten how funny he was. He could always make her laugh. They talked about old times, people they'd known, the wine easing any residue of awkwardness that might have initially existed. She hadn't enjoyed herself so much in ages. She could be totally herself with Greg because of their shared history and when she caught him holding her glance for a little too long in a few unguarded moments, she felt flattered, enjoying the flirtatious element underpinning their conversation. There was no harm in it, she told herself. It no longer meant anything. Just a bit of harmless fun.

She was suddenly aware of the diners thinning out and the waiters hovering and glanced at her watch. It was eleven thirty. Time had flown. She'd chosen well. The ambience was relaxed, not too intimate. The food was simple French fare at its best and plenty of it. She remembered Greg had a hearty appetite. Nouvelle cuisine was not for him. She wanted to split the bill, but he wouldn't hear of it.

'You can ask me back for a night cap, though.'

The warning bell she should have heard going off in her head, was severely muted by wine-induced recklessness.

As it was a lovely night she declined Greg's offer of a cab and they walked back to the apartment, enjoying the cool night air.

He looked round the cosy living room appreciatively.

'Nice place.'

'Thanks.' She slipped off her jacket.' What would you like? Brandy? Sambucca?'

'You know what,' he said, sitting back and making himself comfortable on the sofa, 'I'd be happy with coffee.'

She crossed to the kitchen, switched on the kettle, lifted down the cafetière and busied herself with the coffee. It was good to have company. When she came back into the room, bearing a tray, he was standing looking at a framed picture of Don on the bureau.

'Good looking guy.'

'I think so.'

It was the first time he'd mentioned Don all evening and she had avoided talking about him too. That way led to pain. Perhaps that was why she had enjoyed herself tonight, not allowing herself to dwell.

Greg sat down beside her on the sofa as she poured.

She was very conscious of him studying her face.

'Can't be easy for you.'

'Nor for him.'

'No, I suppose not,' he said.

'Must help having you to write to.'

He caught the hesitation in her voice as she replied, faintly.

'I suppose so.'

'What does that mean?'

She shrugged, turned away from him. He put his hands gently on her shoulders, turned her round to look at him. Saw the distressed expression on her face.

'Kay? What is it? What's wrong?'

Before she'd thought about it, she found herself pouring out her heart to him, in a way she never had to anyone else, even Janet. Don's letters from prison were always a disappointment. He never discussed his feelings. She explained her theory of post-traumatic stress to Greg. The fact that Don had never sought any help.

'Does post-traumatic stress last all that time? What is it? Six years?' he asked.

'It can, if you don't have any counselling. You bury your emotions.'

'I'm sorry to say this,' he hesitated, 'but couldn't he just have changed? Prison must do that to a man.'

She couldn't bear to think of Don changed. She had built her hopes on counselling being the key to the restoration of the man she knew and loved. She'd even written to the prison authorities suggesting it, but they'd written back stating they couldn't do it without the prisoner's consent. They also pointed out that the kind of intervention she was suggesting was unnecessary, as Don had been considered sane and fit to plead at the time of his trial.

Greg listened gravely. When she'd finished, he took her hand in his. He could see the tears at the edge of her eyes. He hated seeing her so unhappy.

'He's a very lucky guy, having you hanging in there - waiting for him.'

'At times, I feel like letting go.'

'What stops you?'

'I love him,' she said simply.

He sat quietly for a moment. Her words had sunk home, but he wasn't giving up so easily.

'Have you any idea when he'll be released?'

'Officially, in four years, but I reckon he'll only serve another two at most.'

'Kay', he chose his words carefully, 'what if he's like... a different guy? Not the one you got engaged to.'

'I don't allow myself to think about that,' she said honestly.

'Perhaps you should.' His tone was gentle, but firm.

'All I have is hope. Don't take that away from me,' she answered, tearfully.

He pulled her into his arms, hugged her.

'I'm so sorry. I didn't mean to upset you.'

He held her for a few moments, let her go reluctantly.

'All I wanted to say is, if he turns out to be so changed that you don't love him anymore. I'll be there, still hoping.'

She dried her eyes, before she spoke, taken aback at his words and the sincerity behind them.

What about Judy?'

'She's a great girl, but she's not you.'

It was Kay's turn to choose her words carefully.

'Greg, I don't want you to put your life on hold.'

'Why not? You're doing it.'

'There's a difference,' she said gently. 'I love Don.'

'You loved me once,' he said hoarsely.

'But not in the same way. Greg, you're a lovely guy, but I could never marry you.'

'I see.'

His face changed suddenly, as if a light had gone out inside him.

'I'm so sorry.'

'Don't be. I appreciate your honesty.'

He gathered himself together, glanced at his watch.

'It's late. I better be going.'

'Of course. You've got your meetings tomorrow.'

'What?' he said faintly.

'With your suppliers.'

'I made that up. Sorry. I don't have any suppliers in New York. It was an excuse to see you.'

She didn't know what to say. He stood up.

'I thought there was still something between us, you know, when you came home for the christening,' he said ruefully. 'Thought I'd give it one more shot. How wrong can you be?'

He kissed her gently on the cheek, crossed to the door and let himself out.

Chapter sixty-one

Kay sat idly gazing out of the window, not really taking in the view as houses flashed by. Being on the commuter belt the Friday night train was pretty busy. A young guy in a studded leather jacket with **LOVE** and **HATE** tattooed on his knuckles was squashed up beside her. Obviously the indecisive type, she mused. She could hear the relentless beat of an unrecognisable rock band escaping from the earphones clamped to his ears. She was forced to surf the waves of sound, an unwilling participant in his activity as he sat, eyes shut, moving his head ever so slightly in time to the beat.

The sky was grey and murky. It had rained steadily during the night. She had not being sleeping too well lately. She had never really got used to the absence of Don's comforting presence in the bed beside her. Neither had she been able to forget her conversation with Greg a few weeks earlier. She lay awake night after night mulling over his words. What if Don never got back to being the guy she'd agreed to marry? Six years apart was a long time. What if he had genuinely fallen out of love with her? She had awakened at three am in their apartment having had an erotic dream involving Greg. It was like a continuation of their night out except that he had stayed behind and they were making love. She was locked in his arms, everything else forgotten.

She had awakened with a start, aroused and ashamed. She put it down to loneliness. She'd being living the life of a nun for the past six years. Didn't know how much more she could take. When she'd called her friend Julie in Scotch Plains for their weekly catch up, Julie had detected an untypical note of depression in Kay's voice. The two young women had known each other since nursery school; had gone through High school together. She felt worried about Kay and invited her for the weekend, using the excuse that she would be alone with the boys, as her husband, Ryan, was at a seminar in San Diego.

Kay found her eyes closing with the steady motion of the train. She thought of the last trip she and Don had made together to Scotch Plains. She kept seeing him in her mind as he sat cross-legged on the floor of the playroom in their friends' big ranch-house style home, playing with Julie and Ryan's two little boys, Luke and Matthew, two and four years old at the time. The three of them had been totally absorbed in creating interesting configurations with the boy's wooden train tracks, swooping bridges, intersecting junctions. The boys loved Don, the way in which he introduced imaginative play. She could hear police cars and ambulances being added to the mix, little Matthew excitedly keeping up a steady commentary. That had been only a month before the crash, before Don's parents were killed. Kay and Don had willingly agreed to babysit as Julie and Ryan were going to a business function in New York, and were staying over for a weekend break at the Waldorf. She remembered the boys sleepily coming into their parents' room in the morning and clambering delightedly onto the bed where Don and Kay were just coming to. The boys snuggled under the bedclothes with them, obviously a weekend routine with their parents as the four of them watched early morning cartoons together. It had been a wonderful weekend and they found themselves envying their friends and looking forward to their own marriage and having kids. Now she felt, helplessly, that if Don didn't appeal against his sentence soon, by the time he got out of prison she would be in her late thirties, with a diminishing chance of having a family. They both loved kids. The thought of marriage without them really saddened her.

As the train drew into Fanwood Station, she tried to brighten up when she saw Julie on the platform; the two boys excitedly trying to catch a glimpse of her through the train windows. They ran down the platform and hurled themselves at her. Matthew's first words 'Where's Uncle Don?' were like salt in her wound. His ten year old brother Luke said nothing. He'd noticed in the past that when he'd asked his parents when Uncle Don was coming back from working in Scotland, they exchanged a glance before answering. He didn't know why, but he knew not to go there.

. . . .

Kay was enjoying herself. They had taken the boys swimming and to a local baseball game. She even cheered on Matthew in a school soccer match. The constant activity kept her from dwelling on her situation. She was glad on the Saturday night when Julie rented a girlie movie and they sat in the living room enjoying a Chinese take away with the boys tucked up in bed. As the film came to an end Julie refilled Kay's wine glass and topped up her own.

'This is terrific. Like old times,' said Kay suddenly realising she was slurring her words ever so slightly, but not really caring.

'I'm glad,' said Julie. 'It's great having you here. Ryan would have moaned on and on about my movie choice and gone down to the den and watched the baseball.'

'Your boys have got so big,' mused Kay sadly. 'Don won't know them when he gets out.'

'They've not forgotten him. They loved their Uncle Don,' Julie said awkwardly.

'He's not dead,' a sharp note had crept into Kay's voice. 'People always talk to me like I'm a widow.'

'I'm sorry… I didn't mean to…' Julie broke off as she saw her friend's face crumbling. She crossed over to the sofa, put her arm round Kay's shoulder.

'They're right in a way,' said Kay trying to hold back the tears, 'I feel like one. I am grieving… for the years we've lost. It hurts like hell, Julie. It really does.'

She buried her face in Julie's shoulder and wept uncontrollably. Julie patted her back soothingly as if Kay was one of her kids. She had never seen her friend like this. Kay was always the strong one; quick to find the solution to any problem. Julie was at a loss, annoyed at her own failure to find any comforting words.

Chapter sixty-two

Madeline was very distressed. She had been calling for some time now, but no-one had appeared. Ever since breakfast, when an overworked attendant impatiently shoved a pink, undercooked sausage into her mouth, before she could voice her protest, her stomach had been churning. Sunningham Residential Nursing left a lot to be desired. 'You get what you pay for,' as her Mother used to say. Sunningham was cheaper than Riverdale, but still cost plenty. Despite that, her room was considerably more down-market than her previous one. Faded grandeur, verging on shabby. She could have put up with that, but not with the inequitable staff ratios. Attendants and nurses were run off their feet. Madeline, who had always been fastidious about her appearance, was wearing the same, stained, blouse she had on the day before. When she complained, the harassed attendant, who dressed her, said her 'stuff' hadn't yet come back from the laundry. Madeline was sure she'd seen one of the residents, wearing an expensive and distinctive cashmere cardigan she'd been given by her agent. She would have to authorise Alan Goodwright to buy her new clothes. His PA could do it and make sure they were properly tagged. He'd protest, of course, at the expenditure. He was already complaining that, for all its shortcomings, Sunningham, was making 'a helluva hole', in her capital. Her stomach gave another ominous rumble, causing her to call out, yet again.

'Nurse! Nurse! For God's sake, Nurse!' she called.

There was a knock at the door.

'Help me, please!' she yelled, with real desperation in her voice.

A tall young woman, she'd never clapped eyes on, appeared.

'Miss Whitney?' she said tentatively. 'Kay Prentice... I wrote to you.'

'Please, tell them I need to go to the toilet.' Madeline's voice betrayed her agitation. 'I've been calling and calling.'

'Right' said Kay, turning on her heel and hurrying out.

She stopped a Nursing Assistant who was helping an old, frail man in pyjamas along the corridor.

'Could someone take Miss Whitney to the toilet, please?'

'She'll just have to take her turn, honey,' the woman replied, not unkindly, 'I've only got one pair of hands.'

'But she's desperate,' Kay explained.

'They's all desperate.'

The assistant turned into a room, the old man teetering at the turn, despite the strong arm round him.

'Tell her I'll be right along, soon as I've dealt with Billy here.'

Kay turned back and tapped Madeline's door, before putting her head round the door.

'Someone will be with you in a minute.'

'Thank you,' said Madeline, gratefully.

Kay withdrew discreetly and stood in the corridor. What was she doing here? she asked herself. What did she hope to achieve? The Nursing Assistant was as good as her word. She bustled along the corridor and disappeared into Madeline's room. Greg's words had struck home with Kay. What if Don wasn't the same? So changed that she couldn't love him anymore? She had to find some way of getting through to him? She thought perhaps Madeline was the key. She'd mulled it over for ages. Perhaps it was the email from her sister, Clare, telling her of Greg and Judy's engagement and their forthcoming marriage in the Fall that had precipitated her current action. Madeline's door suddenly opened, interrupting her reverie.

'You can come in now. She's all ready for you.'

The Assistant tucked a blanket around Madeline's knees.

'There you go, honey. And don't worry 'bout it, next time. You's all padded up.'

She left in a flurry of disinfectant and air freshener.

Madeline broke the awkward silence.

'Sorry about that, Miss Prentice.'

'Oh, don't apologise.'

'This is my third nursing home. They seem to get progressively more short-staffed.'

'Thank you for seeing me,' said Kay.

'Did you expect me to refuse?'

'I wouldn't have blamed you if you had.'

'Because your fiancé put me here?' There was bitterness in her tone.

'Miss Whitney,' said Kay, carefully. 'Don is a decent, gentle guy. What he did to you is… incomprehensible.'

'So he's asked you to apologise on his behalf?' There was barely concealed anger in her voice. 'A bit late for that.'

'He doesn't know I'm here.'

If Madeline was surprised to hear this, it didn't register.

'Look,' Kay continued urgently, 'they said he was sane at the time, but they were wrong. He was suffering some kind of post-traumatic stress. I know that. You must understand what he'd been through…'

'If you've come to berate me over the circumstances of his birth,' Madeline interrupted 'you can leave now.'

'I haven't. I'm just trying to make you understand. He'd had so many knocks. First of all, there was the car crash. He blamed himself for his parent's death.'

Madeline waved a hand imperiously, stopping Kay in mid-flow.

'Why are you telling me this?'

'I need you to help him.' Kay's voice was breaking. 'Please! You've got to.'

A look of emotional pain crossed over Madeline's face.

'I'm the last person he'd want help from,' she said quietly, 'Now would you please leave.'

But Kay was determined. 'Let me explain,' she continued

urgently 'finding out he'd survived a termination was the culmination of a number of very traumatic...'

'Nurse!' Madeline's shout cut across Kay's words. 'I don't want to talk about this. Just go. Leave me alone.'

Kay crossed resignedly to the door. She'd tried, but she'd half-expected this reaction. She turned round, wearily.

'You know, you're just like him,' she said quietly. 'He won't talk about it either. Now I know where he gets it from.'

Tears sprung into Madeline's eyes. The emotion caught her by complete surprise. She thought she was incapable of feeling anything but justified self-pity. As Kay opened the door to leave, she was stopped in her tracks by the unexpected hint of pleading in Madeline's voice.

'Miss Prentice... please.'

Kay stopped and turned back.

Chapter sixty-three

Whatever Kay had said, she seemed to have opened the floodgates as far as Madeline Whitney was concerned. The girl sat there listening while Madeline talked about things she'd shut away inside herself. Her early struggle back in England. Her Polish father's opposition to her career choice. His feeling that to pursue an acting career was living in a fantasy world and her determination to prove him wrong. Long periods of unemployment and constant rejection followed. Then she met the man who fathered Don. Kay wondered when Madeline was going to mention him. The preamble before seemed like some kind of self-justification. She'd met him while doing a television play. She'd seen him in a lot of television productions, not exactly a household name, but an actor in demand who made a good living. He was playing a murderer in this particular production. She was one of his victims. He'd sat beside her in the chuck wagon. They'd got talking. She asked his advice on her career. He was helpful, open and friendly. When he asked if they could meet up for a drink, she happily agreed. She started seeing a lot of him. He was the first man she'd ever slept with. It wasn't till shortly afterwards that he confessed he was married with two children. She felt utterly betrayed. Told him to stay out of her life. It was a painful split. Her first West End break came just at the right time. She'd hoped the excitement of a leading role would stop the pain of separation from the man she loved, despite everything. It didn't. When he appeared in her dressing-room one night after the show, she couldn't wait for her other visitors to leave, before she threw herself into his arms. She saw him for another three months after that, clandestine meetings, which she hated. He talked about leaving his wife, but then, just as suddenly, he disappeared from her life without further explanation. She'd been frantic, sat around her flat for hours, waiting, praying for the phone to ring. She'd even called his house. She hadn't thought it through. She knew she was behaving like a crazy woman, but she needed to hear his voice. When his wife answered, she hung up. When the play transferred to Broadway, she was sure she would hear from him. Even a card offering congratulations, but there was nothing. She'd decided, then, no matter how painful, she would just have to forget him.

'When I found out I was pregnant, I was frantic. Well, not at first. I had some stupid idea that he would leave his wife, come to the States and we'd live happily ever after.' She gave a rueful half-smile.

'He didn't even answer my letters... not till I told him I was going to have an abortion. He sent a brief note with a hundred dollars in it, saying it was the best solution.'

She paused, distressed. 'Best solution for whom?'

Chapter sixty-four

Word had got round. The Creative Writing tutor was hot. Not that Don's fellow inmates were starved of female company. A fair sprinkling of the officers were of the female variety, but fair applied to very few. She was a playwright, apparently. He wasn't too familiar with contemporary Scottish playwrights, but Don enrolled in her class. If he started to write again, perhaps he could lose himself. Time might stop creeping by.

Paula di Maggio was of medium height, slim but shapely. A mass of black curly hair tumbled over her forehead. She was obviously new to this kind of audience. He could see she was pretty nervous. She kept pushing her hair out of her dark brown, intelligent eyes in a repetitive, anxious way. Not that he blamed her. A bunch of guys from E block, the hardliners, had come along. It was doubtful if any of them could write, never mind creatively. She was obviously the attraction. She spent a lot of time outlining the basic precepts of writing, stressing that the best writing came from personal experience.

WRITE WHAT YOU KNOW she chalked up on the blackboard. As she stretched up to pull down the board, her back to the class, one clown, a giant muscle-bound guy called Staples, who usually spent all his free time working out in the gym, stood up and simulated grinding sex in her direction, to the amusement of his E wing stooges. Don felt sorry for her and protective towards her, as she turned round, unsure of what was going on.

'So have you got that?' she asked.

'Oh yeah, baby,' said Staples, a lascivious grin on his face.

'Ok, good,' she said. 'There's pens and paper on your desks. I want you to write about some important event in your life. Some experience that is either happy, sad, life changing, whatever. The important thing to remember is?' She crossed to the board and underlined what she'd written.

'WRITE WHAT YOU KNOW,' they all chanted in unison.

What they knew proved pretty depressing reading. Lives on crack, friends, family members dying from drug overdoses, violent fathers, alcoholic mothers, a whole circle of deprivation and crime. When they stood up to read, haltingly, what they'd written, some of it was so raw and graphic it made Don wince. He felt he had nothing to say that could match this and screwed up his paper after the first sentence.

He had to hand it to Paula Di Maggio, she did not flinch at what she was hearing. Her true feelings were masked under a professional, crisp manner. The writer in her took over, offering praise, constructive criticism and unfailing encouragement. When one harmless looking little guy, known as 'Bam' MacArthur said he had difficulty putting his thoughts on paper, but could 'say the words', she talked about the merits of the oral tradition and invited him to share it with the class. MacArthur sat quietly and in a low monotonous tone, lacking in any form of emotion, he described how he'd murdered his partner. No detail was left out. Don felt physically sick as the little guy graphically described the state of his partner's skull after he'd 'done her in wi a hammer.'

Paula had turned pale, but as the inmates stood up to file out at the end of the session, her composure had returned. The teacher in her took over; she thanked them for their efforts and left them with encouraging words.

As Don made to file past, she stopped him with a smile.

'I had hoped we might have had a contribution from you.'

He looked at her quizzically.

'Being a journalist, you have a big advantage over these men.'

He wondered, for a moment, how she knew his occupation. Of course, his trial had been all over the tabloids. Madeline Whitney was big news, even now. He was, too, by association.

'Conditions here are not exactly ideal for creativity.'

She nodded, sympathetically.

'I know. When I tell people I'm a writer, they invariably say 'Oh, I could write, too, if I had the time.'

'As if that's all it takes,' said Don.

'Exactly.' She smiled again, a flash of understanding between them.

'See you again, next week, I hope.'

Don nodded and filed out.

'You've knocked it off there, big man,' a thin weedy character known as 'wee Oakie', reputed to be a sex offender, leered at him.

'She's pure intae you.'

Don shrugged dismissively. Oakie gave him the creeps. He turned on his heel and walked away.

Chapter sixty-five

It was Kay's second trip to Sunningham. The first one had been a very emotional visit for both she and Madeline. It was obvious to Kay that, like Don, Madeline had locked her true feelings away inside her. Now she was prepared, not only to talk about Don's birth, but to write to him. Obviously, she couldn't write herself, but Kay had offered to do it for her. She'd even brought her laptop. Madeline would dictate.

In the week that had gone past, Kay worried that the star would change her mind. She was convinced that a letter from his mother would be cathartic for Don. She wasn't entirely sure what was going on in his mind, but she was determined not to give up on him. Many of her, so-called, friends were now voicing the fact that they thought her foolish, wasting her life. Even her sisters had gone on about Kay's biological clock ticking relentlessly on. They urged her to start dating again. She should take off her engagement ring and carry on with her life. She'd, half-heartedly, gone out for drinks and dinner with a young Congressman when she was on one of her Washington assignments. Getting ready for the date, she was nervous, edgy. It felt like betrayal. Paul Abrahams was good looking, intelligent and charming. His only problem being, he wasn't Don. She found herself drifting off in the middle of his conversations. 'I'm afraid I'm boring you?' he said at one point. Despite her denials, she was relieved when he didn't ask her out again.

She found Sunningham a depressing place to visit. It made her think of her own mortality. She prayed to God she wouldn't end up in such an institution. Kay wouldn't have blamed Madeline if she'd had second thoughts about the letter. To all intents and purposes, Don was responsible for her incarceration. They were both serving a sentence. The only difference being Don would be eventually released. Madeline's was for life.

The actress was looking pale, bright eyed, but thin. An untouched plate of food sat on the table in front of her. Kay hoped they took time to feed Madeline in this place. Staff shortages and dependent patients were a recipe for trouble. She'd seen a documentary on CNN about patients starving to death in so-called 'care' homes.

'I was too excited to eat today,' Madeline said, as if reading Kay's mind.

'I've been wondering what I'm going to say. How can I make him understand?'

Before Kay could reply, the same attendant, as before, bustled in and took away the plate of food, clucking exasperatedly, before leaving them alone.

'He's very fortunate to have you,' said Madeline suddenly. 'It's when things get tough you know who your friends are. I admire your persistence.'

'I love him,' Kay replied quietly. 'It's as simple as that.'

Chapter sixty-six

Things were a little tense. There had been a rooftop protest the day before, led, surprisingly, by 'Bam' MacArthur. Don hadn't been part of it, but he'd heard the commotion. Some prisoners had lit fires in their cells. He wasn't sure if they had a particular beef. It seemed to be about conditions in general. His fellow inmates fell into different camps. Some who were just inadequate human beings, not fully socialised. Others, whom he felt, had mental health issues and shouldn't be in prison. A third category was the type who never admitted responsibility for his own shortcomings. It was always someone else's fault that he'd turned to crime. Those guys looked for someone to blame at every opportunity. They were like volcanoes, unpredictable, dormant most of the time, but suddenly erupting in a furious outburst. God help anyone in their path! Three of the officers had been assaulted, one seriously. There was to be a public enquiry. In the short term, Don's planned trip to the gym was cancelled, as the protesters had accessed the roof through that area, breaking the skylight window in the process. Instead, he was being sent off to one of the workshops. The powers that be obviously had decided there would be no idle hands that day. He was changing from his gym kit when the vast iron cell door was suddenly unlocked.

'Letter for you.'

A young officer stood there bearing an air mail letter.

'Any chance of the stamp?' My kid's a collector.'

'Sure,' Don said. He looked at the envelope curiously, before tearing off the corner. The name and address were typed. He changed quickly, ready for the workshop call and tore open the envelope. He sank onto the bed when he saw the typed signature, 'Madeline Whitney' and started to read.

'It was the most difficult decision of my life. One that I kept putting off. That's why it was done so late. I kept hoping something

would happen to change my mind, but I had no money. I was struggling to scrape a living. A termination seemed the only way out. The right decision at the time. When I found out you'd survived, the guilt was unbearable. I'd refused to think of you as a baby in order to go through with it.'

He read on, a mass of conflicting emotions.

'I refused to see you because I couldn't bear to think what the consequences of my actions might have been. The only way I have been able to get through my life since, has been by self-deception, refusing to acknowledge that it ever happened

I understand that you must hate me. I only wonder if you can, in time, find it in your heart to forgive me. I have no right to expect your forgiveness, but I pray for it every day.'

Don dropped the letter, convulsed with sobs which wracked his whole body.

Chapter sixty-seven

Madeline's heart sank when she saw the crumbling exterior of Belleview Nursing Home. It had looked a lot better in the brochure; the photographs, no doubt, taken years before. Despite the inadequacies of the previous care home, with the credit crunch, it, also, had proved too expensive. She found the need to constantly move extremely stressful. With her total physical dependence, routine was paramount. She didn't ask much. Someone to bathe, feed, dress her and take her to the toilet.

God knows what she could expect at Belleview. Hopefully, appearances might be deceptive, she told herself.

Even years of acting training failed to hide her dismay, as a faintly seedy guy, in a crumpled uniform, came forward to wheel her out of the taxi, specially adapted for wheelchair use. Madeline preferred to arrange these things herself. Her independent spirit stopped her from phoning friends to arrange her transfer. She had no wish to be a burden to other people. Not that they were falling over one another to help. After the first initial outburst of sympathy and help, the offers of support waned with the passage of years. She wasn't bitter about it. People were busy with their own lives, their own families. Why should they put themselves out for her? 'As you sew, so shall you reap,' she was reminded. She had been so wrapped up in her career and her showbiz life that she had little time to spare for other people. Sure, she'd made charitable contributions to good causes. Signing a cheque was easy. Finding the time in her, hitherto, busy life to visit the sick or needy, was less so.

'Hey, you're Madeline Whitney. I seen all your movies.'

The seedy guy wheeled her up the overgrown path.

'The name's Jake. I'll be looking after you.'

She felt total dismay at the prospect.

'Never thought we'd get someone classy like you at Belleview,' he continued. 'Anything you want, Madeline, you talk to me.'

Chapter sixty-eight

Don's fingers were flying over the keys. The novel was almost writing itself. His only difficulty was keeping up with his own thoughts. Madeline Whitney's letter seemed to have released raw painful emotions, partially eased by writing back to her. He'd written numerous letters to Kay, too. She'd cried with relief when she read them. It was as if she'd got the old Don back. She didn't know whether he'd been receiving any counselling in prison, or whether the contact with Madeline had brought about the change. She was just grateful that he seemed restored to his old self and counted the days to his release. He told her he had an appeal coming up. Thank God he'd pursued it. Until now, he had been indifferent to the idea of release. He seemed to have thought his incarceration was deserved; retribution if you like.

'You know you're not really supposed to do that.'

Don was suddenly aware of Paula Di Maggio looking over his shoulder at what he was typing.

'Do what?'

'Write about your own case.'

'You're the one who went on about 'Write what you know.'

'Yeah, but, apparently, there are prison rules.'

'Saying what exactly?'

'Well, you're not supposed to profit from the proceeds of your crime.'

'I didn't commit any crime.'

'Isn't that what they all say?'

He swallowed hard.

'I may have had vengeance in my heart, when I went backstage that night, but I couldn't harm another human being. It's not in my nature, I know that's easy to say, but it's true,' he said simply... 'I've been beating myself up about it ever since, blaming myself for crippling Madeline Whitney, but at the end of the day, it was an accident. I meant her no harm.'

Something in the intensity of his tone and the honest light in his eyes convinced Paula he was telling the truth. This book was important to him. There was no way she was going to stand in his way.

'Anyway,' he said, grinning, 'with my luck, it'll lie in a publisher's drawer unread, or worse still, in their trash can, so you don't need to worry.'

Chapter sixty-nine

Theresa Dougan looked down lovingly at her little son, as he sucked hungrily at her nipple. She felt regret that she'd bottle fed the three girls. There didn't seem to be the same amount of information on the benefits of breast feeding when the girls were growing up. Anyway, with a husband who spent more time in prison, than at home, convenience was the name of the game. She had to leave bottles with her mother, so that she could do her wee cleaning jobs, in order to put food on the table. Her mother never complained at being landed with constant child minding. Theresa would have preferred it if she had. Instead, she gave Theresa her 'I told you so' looks every time Jimmy landed back in prison. She never wanted Theresa to marry him. The family were a bad lot. Jimmy's father was in and out of jail. His mother was an alcoholic. Theresa couldn't help it. She'd fallen in love with Jimmy Dougan, despite his faults and his family. The Judge, at his last trial, had branded him a recidivist. Jimmy was determined to prove him wrong. Since the birth of his sons, he'd decided to go straight. So far he was sticking to his promise. He'd re-trained as a house painter. Work was slow to come in. In the current recession, people were doing a lot of their own decorating, but they got by. Theresa had got used to managing on very little. As long as the kids had enough to eat and clothes on their backs, she was content.

She pressed the remote on the TV and rubbed the baby's back. The three girls and Kevin, her first boy, were sitting at the table eating fish fingers. Kevin stood up and ran over to the fridge.

'Can I get a yoghourt?'

'Not till you sit back down and finish what's on your plate.'

Kevin pulled his sulky face, but did as he was told. He pushed the food round the plate in a half-hearted fashion. His mother ignored him. He was increasingly attention seeking since the new baby had arrived on the scene.

Suddenly, a picture of Don Creighton flashed up on the screen, which was showing the local BBC news.

Theresa quickly turned up the volume to hear what the newscaster was saying.

'The American journalist, Donald Creighton, involved in the controversial revenge attack on Madeline Whitney seven years ago, was released from Broughton prison today.'

'Jimmy! Jimmy. Quick!' Theresa called out.

Jimmy rushed in from the bedroom in overalls, paint spattered and with paintbrush in hand. Theresa pointed at the TV.

'Look!'

'Jeez! I thought somethin'd happened to the wean,' Jimmy's relief was palpable.

'It's your pal fae inside. The big Yank, look!'

Jimmy turned the sound up even louder to hear the newscaster.

'Questions were raised in Parliament to-day, when it was revealed that sales from Creighton's book, 'Survivor', written while serving his sentence, were set to make him a wealthy man. Concern was expressed that his victim, twice Oscar winner, Madeline Whitney, left with quadriplegia since the attack...'

A picture of Madeline was flashed up on screen.

'is currently living in very strained circumstances in New York.'

Jimmy smiled. 'Told him he wouldnae serve the full ten years.'

The baby's eyes were closing. He was content, sated. Theresa was just putting him down gently in the carry-cot when there was a ring at the door bell. The eldest girl, Debbie, immediately jumped up.

'Tell Kylie you're no' goin' out to play till you've done these dishes,' her mother shouted after her, wearily picking up the dirty plates.

Debbie came back in, a familiar, tall figure in tow. Jimmy, about to resume work in the bedroom, turned to see Don there.

'Fuck's sake!' the wee man grinned, 'We were just lookin' at you on the telly.' The two men hugged, delighted to see one another again.

'Great to see you, big man,' said Jimmy. 'Theresa, get the kettle on.'

'Not for me,' said Don. 'I've a car waiting. Going to the airport.'

'No' even got time for a cup of tea?' asked Theresa.

'Afraid not. I'm being deported.'

'That's a liberty.' Jimmy was genuinely annoyed.

'Undesirable alien. That's me.'

Jimmy grinned. 'Sounds like something outta Star Trek.'

Don crossed to the carry-cot, looked down at the sleeping child, a smile on his face.

'This the new little Dougan?'

'Aye, that's Brendan,' the wee man said proudly.

'Always wanted three boys and three lassies. Only one to go.'

'That will be right!' Theresa said vehemently.

'Don't listen to her,' Jimmy said, sotto voce, to Don, but Theresa had heard.

'I'm telling you,' she said emphatically, 'I'm going to get one of they long flannel nighties wi' a padlock at the bottom.'

The insistent blaring of a car horn drew Don to the window.

'Gotta go.' He hugged Jimmy. 'Listen, man I wouldn't have got through it without you.'

'You take care of yourself, you hear?' The wee man's voice was cracking.

Don smiled at Theresa and the family before Jimmy showed him out. The wee man came back into the room, visibly moved. He crossed to the window.

'Gie him a wave.'

The baby suddenly let out a lusty cry as a pocket of wind disturbed his slumbers. Theresa crossed to the carry cot, pulled back the blanket to pick him up, revealing a fat brown envelope. She picked it up.

'Jimmy!' Her face was astonished.

Jimmy turned round. Theresa had opened the envelope to reveal bundles of £50 pound notes. They looked at one another, hardly able to believe their luck.

Chapter seventy

Don couldn't believe he was back on American soil. He felt like emulating Pope John Paul by kissing the tarmac, so relieved was he to be in New York. There had been delays over his extradition and confusing, contradictory, press releases, for which he was grateful. Most of the paparazzi had given up waiting. He was able to brush past the few persistent ones with a 'no comment,' exiting the airport, bag in hand before getting into a cab.

'Belleview Nursing Home in Queens,' he instructed the driver.

The guy sped off while cameras flashed through the windows. Don held up a newspaper to hide his face. He felt slightly mean, being a journalist himself. These guys had to make a living, but, right now, he didn't want it to be at his expense. He wished to put the past behind him. Start afresh, but first, some unfinished business. He paid off the taxi and walked up the weed strewn path to the entrance. Despite Kay having warned him, he was still shocked to find Madeline had been reduced to a place like this. He rang the bell. A face appeared at one of the upstairs windows, peering out from behind a greying curtain. He wasn't sure whether it was a man or a woman. The curtain was quickly replaced. He rang the bell again. Heard the sound of shuffling feet. The door opened slowly. A neglected looking old man in soiled pyjamas, stood there, peering out from behind thick glasses, the legs of which were held together with band-aid.

'Is that my cab?'

The sleazy looking attendant, Jake, suddenly appeared behind him, looking annoyed. He ignored Don and grabbed the old man by the elbow and spun him round.

'What you doing out of bed, Henry?'

Not waiting for a reply, he started to lead the old man away.

'Madeline Whitney?' Don called after his retreating back.

'Day room,' Jake replied, without breaking his stride.

The old man had to increase his faltering steps to a run to keep up with him.

The first thing that hit Don was the smell.

How could anyone live with that? Worse was yet to come. When he looked into the Day Room, he was reminded of the pit of horror scene from Gorky's *The Lower Depths*.

At first he found it hard to recognise Madeline from the woman he'd seen before. She seemed to have shrunk and was pitifully thin. She was sitting amongst an elderly group of patients, eyes closed. Many of them appeared in various stages of dementia. One woman was rocking backwards and forwards. Another was beating her hand rhythmically. Several were shouting for a nurse. There was no sign of any staff. Childish cartoons played on a TV, which nobody was watching. Don crossed over to where Madeline was sitting, called to her gently,

'Madeline... Madeline!'

She didn't seem to hear him. Her eyes remained closed.

He bent down so that he was level with her ear.

'Mom,' he said, his voice choked with emotion.

Madeline slowly opened her eyes. She looked at him blankly for a moment, then, with dawning realisation, her eyes filled with tears. He took her in his arms. A long emotional hug.

'We're going home,' he whispered.

Chapter seventy-one

Kay was singing along to the car radio. It was a beautiful summer's day; good to be alive. She couldn't believe how quickly events had moved along since Don's release. It was as if he felt his life had been on hold for the past seven years. In a way it had been. He'd only been back weeks and already they'd set the date for their wedding, only three months away. It was going to be a small affair. The important thing for them was not to waste any more time. They wanted kids and were already having fun trying.

She expected Don to have changed and he had. She knew you couldn't spend six years in prison and emerge unscathed. He seemed like a man on a mission. Intent on getting things done as quickly as possible, as if every moment was precious, as indeed it was to him. They'd always talked about a house in the Hamptons. A pipe dream, of course, until now. The success of *Survivor*, his novel, had made all things possible. It had even led to a three book deal.

Kay got out of the car. The house still took her breath away. She had spotted it online, but it was even more stunning in reality. Its beautiful lawn led almost to the water's edge. She would never tire of the view. As she walked up the path, the middle-aged housekeeper opened the door.

'They're on the patio, Kay,' Mrs Price smiled welcomingly.

Kay passed through the beautiful panelled hallway, noting again the sweep of the magnificent staircase. She knew from the plans they'd pored over, a perfect nursery would be up those stairs, just off the master bedroom. Hardly containing her excitement, she hurried through the cool, elegant lounge with its large picture windows, marvelling again at the breathtaking view over the water, then crossed to the patio doors. She stopped abruptly at the doorway as she took in the scene.

Don was sitting in the sunshine, by his mother's wheelchair.

Madeline had a napkin round her neck. He was feeding her gently, as if she was his child, wiping her mouth carefully. Kay's eyes filled with tears.

Acknowledgements

To my Literary Agent, Brendan Davis, of Film Rights Ltd. who urged me to turn my Film Screenplay, Flesh And Blood, into a novel, as Hollywood was 'buying up books'. In order to encourage me, he sent me an application for the Dundee International Book prize, for which this novel was on the initial short-list.

To my late brother-in-law, Dr. John Morrow, who provided me with invaluable medical advice re Madeline's injuries.

To Glasgow Common Purpose, who invited me on their year long programme as a representative of the Arts. The contacts and help I received from the Prison Service and Judiciary, in particular, gave me enormous insight into prison life and Judicial procedure.

To Nick Broadhead of SNB Publishing Ltd, for his supreme editorial and technological skills.

And to my late brother, Jim Delaney, for his background knowledge and support.

Last, but not least, to my wonderful young grandson, Gregory Campbell, for his invaluable computer know-how, willingness to help, and infinite patience with the many gaps in my technological ability.

About the author

Anne Downie is a native of Glasgow, Scotland. She has a grown up son and daughter and two fantastic young grandsons, Matthew and Gregory.

An actor and award-winning writer, she is a graduate of Glasgow University and trained at The Royal Scottish Academy Of Music and Drama. She has worked in TV as a Drama Script Editor and Story-liner and as Writer in Residence at Dundee Rep's Youth Theatre.

Her many plays have been performed throughout Scotland and in Ireland.

She has written extensively for TV and BBC radio.

As an actor, she has performed at The National Theatre in London and in most theatres in Scotland. Her performances cover a wide range of work, from Pantomime (with the legendary Stanley Baxter) and Classical Theatre, to TV Stand-up Comedy on Channel 4's Halfway to Paradise.

She has also appeared in numerous TV Dramas over the years. Her most recent acting performances have been in films.

Printed in Great Britain
by Amazon